THE WORLD THROUGH YOUR EYES

GUERNICA WORLD EDITIONS 44

VALERIA CAMERINO

THE WORLD THROUGH YOUR EYES

TORONTO—CHICAGO—BUFFALO—LANCASTER (U.K.)
2022

Guernica Editions Founder: Antonio D'Alfonso

Michael Mirolla, general editor
Françoise Vulpé, editor
Interior and cover design: Errol F. Richardson

Guernica Editions Inc.
287 Templemead Drive, Hamilton (ON), Canada L8W 2W4
2250 Military Road, Tonawanda, N.Y. 14150-6000 U.S.A.
www.guernicaeditions.com

Distributors:
Independent Publishers Group (IPG)
600 North Pulaski Road, Chicago IL 60624
University of Toronto Press Distribution (UTP)
5201 Dufferin Street, Toronto (ON), Canada M3H 5T8
Gazelle Book Services, White Cross Mills
High Town, Lancaster LA1 4XS U.K.

First edition.
Printed in Canada.

Legal Deposit—First Quarter
Library of Congress Catalog Card Number: 2021949320
Library and Archives Canada Cataloguing in Publication
Title: The world through your eyes / Valeria Camerino.
Names: Camerino, Valeria, author.
Series: Guernica world editions ; 44.
Description: Series statement: Guernica world editions ; 44
Identifiers: Canadiana (print) 20210357150 | Canadiana (ebook) 20210357207 | ISBN
9781771836920 (softcover) | ISBN 9781771836937 (EPUB)
Subjects: LCGFT: Literature.
Classification: LCC PR6103.A4 W67 2022 | DDC 823/.92—dc23

I wish I could show you
when you are lonely or in darkness,
the astonishing light of your own being.
—Hafez of Shiraz

To my daughter,
the reason why I cherish the past,
enjoy the present,
and look forward to the future

PROLOGUE

I was lying in my bed, feeling cosy under the weight of the blankets as I listened to the sound of rain pouring down at dawn. The robins were singing to announce the start of the day. It was the beginning of spring, my favourite time of the year. Spring is all about renewal, rebirth, closing a chapter and making a fresh start, and it is no coincidence that the Iranian New Year, *Nowruz*, occurs at the spring equinox. Was there a better time to leave the past behind once and for all, and never look back?

These were my thoughts as I stared at the trees in full bloom through my window.

I had been waiting too long for a big change that would save me from myself and my sense of failure. It was time to act, to be that change.

I had been focusing all my efforts on trying to forget a past which was too burdensome to be swept under the carpet. But the harder I was trying to forget and forgive myself in the process, the clearer it would come back to life inside my head, holding my dreams hostage, sucking all my vital energies, forcing me to live in an eternal limbo where time and space had no defined boundaries.

That was it. There was no more time to waste. No more space for regrets, for impossible questions that could never be answered, for all those hours spent staring at a mirror which reflected an image you could not recognise. Was that really *you? Where had you been when life was happening just in front of your eyes?*

I took a blank piece of paper and started making a list. I kept scribbling down ideas until my fingers hurt.

I had achieved so much in my young life, but that was still not enough. I was born with this constant need to test my own limits, to cross that invisible line that separates the ordinary from the extraordinary. My adrenaline addiction pushed me to always want more. I wanted to live more intensely, to love more deeply, to laugh harder, to cry with joy, to experience new ways of life.

That was probably what had encouraged me to sign up for that flamenco class, because I needed to channel my energy into something constructive. Because being a passionate person is a blessing and a curse at the same time. Passion can destroy you day after day. I knew that all too well.

Though I also knew that there was nothing I could do to contain that flame burning inside my soul.

Inside of me, there were two worlds that peacefully coexisted most of the time, although, on some occasions, they could revolt against each other.

The world which everybody could see was made of school runs, doctor's appointments, swimming lessons, tax bills, parents' evenings, interviews, and press conferences.

The other one was shielded from public view, and from public judgement too. It was a world made of dreams and passionate emotions, art and creativity, impulse and desire. It was an intimate space where my free spirit could thrive. Where there were no rules to conform to, no expectations to be fulfilled, no deadlines to be met. It was just me and my wandering mind, which was free to run wild and discover places that only those who questioned the mainstream view could access.

But everything changed the day I met Miad.

From a young age, my restless spirit had gotten me into trouble. I would look for that feeling of love and affection I was desperately craving in the wrong places, with the wrong people—emotionally dry, unaffectionate, and self-centred individuals totally incapable of loving anybody other than themselves.

But the thrill of being with someone who could offer no certainties other than a mind-blowing roll in the hay was truly addictive. And like any adrenaline junkie, I could not do without the emotional rollercoaster that those impromptu encounters would trigger. I *needed* that to feel alive, to prove my own existence.

It was very clear to me: If I could not feel strongly enough, I would be dead inside.

Sex was the cure but also the disease. Because for someone as emotional as myself, it was impossible to sleep with someone without getting emotionally involved. It was going against my own nature. And you can lie to anybody, but you cannot lie to yourself.

Whether it was a friendship or something more, I was looking for a deeper connection. I could *feel* people, absorb their emotions, and make them mine. I had no filters, no barriers.

I was there, exposed to the world in all my vulnerability, and indeed, that was my strongest armour.

I was well aware that men found my personality charming and intriguing. There was something intrinsically sexual about the way I walked, the tone of my voice, the way I looked straight into someone's eyes without ever lowering my gaze, my contagious laugh, the sophisticated image I liked to project. It was empowering to stand out from the crowd, knowing that I could seduce any man I wanted in the blink of an eye. In those moments, I would feel invincible. The awareness that few men could resist my charm was a reassuring thought. It would make me feel in control, the author of my own destiny on a path of self-destruction.

But life is unpredictable, and most things are totally out of our control.

Like falling in love.

For most people, falling in love is a temporary phase in which one gradually loses their common sense. It is inebriating and intoxicating at the same time. But for someone like me, that phase could last forever. I could fall in love every day, but not necessarily with a person. I could see love all around me.

The first night we met, a strange feeling pierced my stomach. I heard an inner voice telling me that you would be part of my life for a very long time. No prediction had ever been more accurate. Because even after you left, the thought of you continued to haunt me like a ghost, and still does.

What first attracted me to you were your eyes. They were the eyes of someone who had lived intensely just like me, who despite the anger and pain, still carried a zest for life. I could tell those eyes had shed lots of tears. But, like a fighter who refuses to surrender in a battle, they were still smiling defiantly. I could lose myself in them. I loved watching how they changed colour, like the many shades of your personality. How those eyes would light up each time we met, as the smile on your face would form wrinkles all around them.

What really made me fall for you, though, was your unique character.

You were so different. You were only thirty-six, yet, whenever I was next to you, I felt I was with a man who knew so much about life. A man tormented by his regrets, who had to take on many responsibilities from a young age, even though his delicate and sensitive nature had not prepared him for that.

There were times when you would allow me to catch a glimpse of your broken soul, to see you fragile and vulnerable in front of my eyes, to let go of the walls you had built all around you not to get hurt.

These were the moments I cherished most. There is nothing more attractive than someone who is not afraid of showing his own weaknesses, to lie there in your bed completely naked and defenceless.

I was making love to someone who still had to come to terms with his past, who was in a constant struggle between his inner child and his responsibilities as an adult, between his own impulses and desires, and what society expected of him, who could be sweet and tender one moment, and harsh and tough the next. It was exhausting, unsettling, and challenging, yet so fascinating.

When I looked at you, I could see myself. That sense of frustration stemming from the feeling of being constantly misunderstood, for being judged *wrong* just because I did not want to conform and settle for anything less than what I aspired to.

A person cannot escape from any negative emotions they experience in life. They must accept them, live them, process them, and only *then* can they let them go. But if that does not happen, they come back to haunt them over and over again.

We could understand each other because we bore the same scars that living in a dysfunctional family leaves on the soul. But the common ground that brought us together in the first place would drive us apart later down the line.

We were on fire. You were angry at the entire world, which you were blaming for all the anger you had towards yourself. I was happy and content on the outside but, deep down, I also struggled to come to terms with an overwhelming feeling of guilt fuelled by failing to meet others' expectations and my own. And for a perfectionist like me, that was totally unacceptable.

We were both hiding behind busy lives to avoid facing our own demons.

Every time I would open that door and see you there, my heart would race like that of a teenager. I would breathe in your crisp scent and lose myself in those tight embraces that would last an eternity. Nothing else would exist in those perfect moments. Just me and you and an irresistible desire to rip each other's clothes off. I wanted to make you mine and possess your mind, as much as I wanted to feel yours. I had no doubt that we belonged to each other.

But you wanted the same—to control my mind and manipulate my emotions. You wanted my own happiness to depend on your every word and mood swing. You wanted to be in charge and set the rules of the game. And the more you would distance yourself and set boundaries between us, only to try and win me back every time I would take back control of my life, the more I would crave your presence, as if my whole existence depended on those random rendezvous.

They say you cannot miss something that had never been yours in the first place. That may be true, but when I looked straight into your eyes, when I stroked every inch of your skin, when I played with your hair and bit your ear, when we were talking, laughing, crying, eating, sweating, fighting, and dreaming about a future we would never share, in that king size bed, our entire world … you were mine.

Tahir

CHAPTER ONE

Once, a friend told me: "You like warriors, not kings." And he was right. You are my warrior, a warrior that makes me feel like a princess. I love who I am when we are together, that silly smile on my face, how you get excited over little things, the way you manage to be so manly and, at the same time, to get embarrassed like a teenager.

Above all, I love how adorable the two of you look while playing together, all the small attentions you give us every day, the feeling of calm and safety your arms give me ... as if I didn't have a care in the world.

I never thought I could have said those three words again. Never say never.

I don't know what the future holds for us. But if I close my eyes, I see you are part of it.

Happy birthday!

Sofia

Sometimes life teases us in the most extraordinary ways. You were born on Valentine's Day. There is no greater paradox than for someone with a narcissistic personality to be born on the day that celebrates love in its purest and most selfless form. But when I scribbled that note, on the inside cover of the book I never gave you, I was still firmly convinced that my unconditional love would have saved you, even from yourself.

When we met, I was all over the place. I had just gone through a painful divorce with the man I considered the love of my life and was trying to make ends meet working as a freelance journalist. I had moved to Yorkshire the year before, after spending nearly ten years living in the Middle East with my then husband and changing jobs every six months or so. I was exhausted, heartbroken, and disillusioned, but also keen to make peace with my past once and for all, forgive myself for my mistakes, and start a new chapter. I was rediscovering myself and was open to the infinite possibilities that life can offer us if we are willing to seize them. I was ready to take a chance, to live new experiences that would have turned those painful moments into faded memories.

I did not even feel like socialising that night, absorbed as I was in my own thoughts, but being around people was the only way to escape the images that were crowding my mind. I liked listening to people opening up their hearts over a glass of wine or two, sharing their daily woes and showing their vulnerabilities. It made me relate to them in a more intimate way, because, at the end of the day, no matter where we are from, how old we are, or how much we earn, we are all just humans trying to figure out life.

The bar was loud and overcrowded, but nothing else caught my attention other than your eyes. They looked sad and shiny, like you had just cried. Still, you smiled at me from across the room and that tiny gesture had the power to warm up my heart.

I smiled back and you walked towards me. Months later, you would tell me how sexy I looked in that red lace dress, my dark, elusive eyes hiding behind a teardrop mahogany fringe.

We talked through the night, although I soon realised that my relentless energy was making you uncomfortable. You wanted to be in control, whereas with me, you were feeling defenceless. You kept asking questions for which you were not patient enough to hear the answer, as your eyes darted around warily.

But to my surprise, you remembered every single detail I had told you, from my birthday to my daughter's name to the size of my shoes. I was impressed.

"My friends always say I look distracted, but in reality, I do listen carefully," you said in your defence.

Then you went on talking about your childhood in Iran. How, one day, you and your siblings had thrown your violent father out of the house after years of physical and emotional abuse towards the family. How the lack of a father figure had marked you and made you grow up quickly given that, as the only man in the household, you felt responsible for your sisters and your mum.

How your eldest sister had helped you move from Tehran to the UK when you were just eighteen, as she hoped that would rescue you from a drug addiction that had already taken away so many young lives. How you were earning a living working as a mechanic.

How you kept changing your views about the world every few years. "I think that is very good," I remember telling you. "That means you are an intelligent guy. Only stupid people never change their minds."

We talked about Iranian politics and society, and how I had developed a strong interest in them after living in Dubai for many years, a city many Iranians called home. I told you about the books I had read about Iran. My favourite one was *City of Lies: Love, Sex, Death, and the Search for Truth in Tehran* by Ramita Navai, which explored the lives of ordinary Tehranis, forced to have many different faces to preserve their true selves.

You agreed with that interpretation, and I promised I would give you a copy of the book later in the week for you to read.

I told you *my* story. How I had also left my hometown, Rome, when I was eighteen, to pursue a degree in the UK. How leaving everything behind was scary and unsettling at first but then turned out to be the best decision of my life, the only possible path to becoming the independent, determined, and strong woman I was today. Someone I was proud to be.

I told you how I had decided to become a journalist when I was eight years old, driven by my strong sense of justice and a compulsive desire to make a difference in this world.

My stubbornness, combined with a sense of duty my parents had instilled in me since a young age, had done the rest. I could never give up on something until I had achieved what I wanted. And that principle, unfortunately, also applied to people. So, after graduating in foreign languages, I had decided to pursue a master's degree in international journalism.

That was a life-changing year for me. Not only because I had the opportunity to share my passion for journalism with like-minded people and learn all the basics of this amazing profession from a wonderful human being, friend, and mentor who soon became a source of inspiration and admiration. But also because that was the year that I met the man who would become my husband and the father of my child.

It was February 2007, and I was halfway through my master's course. A fellow coursemate had convinced me to attend a speed-dating event organised by the International Student Society for Valentine's Day.

I was not in the mood for partying after being dumped a few weeks before by a professional badminton player who had waited until the day after my birthday to tell me he had no strong feelings for me. The emotionless expression he wore as he said those words, just a day after he had celebrated my special day with romantic gestures, showering me with gifts and taking me out to dinner, hit me like a bucket of ice-cold water. But I put on a brave face and filled a bin bag with all his stuff, and when he came to collect it, I handed the bin bag to him and shut the door in his face, without paying any attention to his puzzled expression. Life was too short to waste it dwelling on the past, or so I was trying to tell myself.

My friend, however, was very persuasive. "It is going to be fun," she said. "We are just going there for a laugh."

Yes, that was the deal. As we walked into town to the event venue, I told her, "Fair enough, I am going there to have a good time. I certainly do not expect to meet the man of my dreams tonight."

Karma is a bitch, they say.

There was a total of ten girls and nine boys. Each of us had two minutes to get to know each other before the boys would move onto the next table.

Two minutes?!? That is ridiculous, I thought, as I sat down at my table holding a glass of Diet Coke in my hand. *How the hell are you supposed to find out anything about a person in just two minutes?*

It turned out I was wrong.

The first few boys were a little weird. *I knew this was a terrible idea,* I told myself.

One of them, a Finnish IT student, used up the time enquiring about a Finnish-Egyptian friend of mine I had mentioned to him as an ice breaker. As if, had I provided enough details, he might have ascertained if he knew him.

But just when I had started giving up hope, *he* was sitting across from me.

He was very shy, like he had never been in a similar situation before. That is to say, in a bar full of people of the opposite sex. He was wearing a baseball cap which partly hid his innocent eyes. There was something very pure and naïve about his look, something that I found irresistibly attractive. I just could not stop staring at him, and that in turn, made him even more uncomfortable.

For some unknown reason, he assumed I was Russian. He told me he had come there with his friend. They were both Omanis.

"Oman?!? Where is that?" I asked, intrigued. I had never heard of his country before.

"It is near Dubai," he replied confused. "Have you heard of that?"

I had indeed, although I still could not locate it on the map. Geography was not among my favourite subjects at school, and anyway, in those years, it was mainly centred around the West.

We were just about to talk about the things we liked to do in our spare time, when the bell rang, reminding us that the two minutes were up, and we were meant to switch partners.

"They do not even give us time to breathe," he said, smiling.

How cute was that? I thought. That was it. I was lovestruck that very moment.

I spent the rest of the evening trying to learn more about this mysterious guy who behaved as if he had just arrived from another planet.

I spotted him sitting on a sofa after the game was over. I walked up to him and sat on the armrest.

"You don't drink alcohol, do you?" I asked, noting that—like myself—he was having a soft drink.

"No," he replied.

"Neither do I," I said. "Are you a Muslim?" I pressed him, eager to find out more.

"Yes, I am," he answered politely, although I could sense that my intrusive questions were making him uneasy.

Some of us were going clubbing afterwards, so I invited him and his friend to join in. He agreed, but when, half an hour later, I could not spot him among the group of people who had followed us from the speed dating bar, I panicked, as I scanned the crowd in search of his mysterious eyes.

Who was he? How could he vanish just like that? And above all, what was that something about him that attracted me so much?

And then, just as I had started to resign myself to the idea that he had just been a product of my imagination, I saw him. He was accompanied by the same friend who had attended the dating event with him, but this time we introduced ourselves properly.

As soon as he saw me, his friend kissed me on both cheeks. I was surprised by such a warm display of affection which, although customary among Southern Europeans, as far as I was aware, was inappropriate in Muslim cultures.

I was even more surprised when Rashid—that's how his friend was called—asked for my number; but I did give it to him, hoping that he had been instructed to do so by my crush, who was just too shy to ask for the number himself.

We all danced through the night; all the while I was trying to make eye contact and catch a glimpse of *his* smile, but every time our eyes would meet for a second or two, he would look away.

All I could gather that night is that his name was Tahir, whose Arabic meaning suggests purity and innocence, two attributes that seemed to be perfectly in tune with his appearance and manner.

He had taken a year off work to study in the UK, attending a mechanical engineering course at the university which would convert his diploma into a degree.

As I found out later, some students from the Gulf countries were funded by their own governments through a scholarship programme, but he was paying for his studies with his own savings.

After obtaining a diploma in Fire and Safety, he had been working as an oilfield engineer in Oman, Yemen, and Saudi Arabia on twelve-hour shifts in the middle of the desert where summer temperatures can exceed fifty degrees Celsius. As he explained, it was an extremely stressful job, mentally and physically, and I wondered how his slim body and reserved personality could have coped with that.

When I got back home that night, I had trouble falling asleep. I felt edgy and inebriated by the loud music, which contrasted with his soft-spoken voice. I replayed the evening in my head, trying to recall each single detail: his scent, which smelled like freshly laundered cotton, his perfectly shaven caramel-brown beard, his tanned skin, our brief conversation.

Two days later, while I was studying at home on a Saturday afternoon, working on an assignment that I was due to hand in the following Monday, the phone rang. I picked up, and Rashid was on the other end of the line.

"Hi! How are you today?" he said, introducing himself.

"I am fine, thanks," I replied, trying to hide my disappointment.

We chatted for a few minutes. Then he told me that someone wanted to say hi to me. It was Tahir.

We were both embarrassed as we knew Rashid would hear whatever we were saying, but we agreed to meet for a drink a few days later.

As we sat at a table in my local pub sipping orange juice, I started telling him about my passion for writing, cooking, and travelling. He listened carefully, his eyes fixed on me.

He told me about his family back home, how in his culture the children were responsible for supporting their elderly parents both financially and emotionally; how the tribal community mattered more than the individual, as its members helped each other in every aspect of life; and how marriages between cousins were still very common.

I was fascinated by his tales of a remote land, which in those years was still little known and possibly misunderstood. A place where life was moving at a much slower pace than in the West, following ancient traditions which were passed on from generation to generation.

He came across as very humble and kind-hearted.

We decided to meet again the following evening, on Valentine's Eve. At the end of the night, he walked me back home and left me on the doorstep.

"Good night," he said, in his cute Arabic accent. I gave him an intense look, one expressing a mix of affection and desire, then closed the door behind me. As I walked up the stairs, I received a text: *I wanted to do something tonight, but I couldn't. Still, I had a great time. Happy Valentine's Day!*

I was totally smitten with my charming, handsome, and courteous Arabian prince.

He had rented a two-bedroom flat just above the university building with his older brother, who was studying on the same course as him, but by just weeks after our first date, we had become inseparable. We would spend entire weekends at my place, which I shared with two young female professionals, locked in my bedroom. We would talk for hours on end about politics and religion, comparing our views of the world, and discovering each other's cultures, getting out of the room only to have a shower or to cook together.

I remember telling him about a guy who had shown some interest in me. In hindsight, maybe I was just trying to push him away from me, as I knew from the very beginning that the fact we were from different countries and backgrounds, speaking different languages and practising different religions, was a recipe for disaster, even though I was too much in love to admit it to myself.

But instead of showing any sign of jealousy or getting annoyed, he just replied: "I think I love you."

I was terrified by the idea of losing him. That was why it was better to stop seeing each other. I wanted to settle down in England after finishing my studies. In a few months, he would finish his course and go back to his country, leaving me heartbroken. *This could not work*, I kept telling myself. But once again, he reassured me.

He said he would find a job in the UK, maybe in Scotland, where the oil and gas sector was thriving, and we could get married and live happily ever after.

How naïve we were!

Soon came the first hurdles. News that the son of a former army guy was engaged in an illicit relationship with a Christian girl had reached Muscat, where his family lived.

Then one day, on our way to the cinema, his mum rang.

"*As-salamu alaykum.*" I could hear a sweet childish voice on the other end of the line.

"*Wa alaykumu as-salam*," Tahir replied, smiling.

To date, I don't know exactly what else they did say during that brief conversation. All I know is that, after he hung up, his eyes did not look the same. They were filled with sadness.

"What happened?" I asked warily.

At first, he did not reply. He was quiet, his eyes downcast. Then he looked at me and told me that his siblings had learned about our relationship from his brother and pushed his mother to call him to make him promise that he would end things immediately and go back to Oman.

I could read the disappointment and confusion on his face as he pronounced those words.

I was gutted. I knew that it would have been hard for our families to accept our relationship, but that was worse than I expected. I tried to say something reassuring, but not a single word came out of my mouth. The call had spoiled our date, and we ended up fighting.

One day later, I received an e-mail from him which I wished I had never read. It started by saying that, as much as he loved me, he could not see a future between us. He could not marry me and make me his wife.

I cried all night. I felt like someone had ripped out my heart.

But then, after a whole day of mourning, I told myself he was right; that we were not meant to be together. I ran a hot bubble bath, put on a nice dress, and went out for a meal with the girls. *A little TLC is all I need*, I thought.

He called incessantly for the following forty-eight hours, but, as much as I was fighting against my own feelings, I did not answer. *Let him go*, my friends would tell me.

But those were just empty words for someone who was deeply in love. I could not escape. I was disappointed and angry at him for letting me go so easily, but all of me was longing to look into his limpid hazel eyes again.

On the third day, I surrendered, and we met outside the library.

"I don't want this to end," he said bluntly, without paying attention to the crowds of students making their way to their lessons.

"I am not sure I can trust you again," I replied. "It will take time."

That was it. We went for a bowling game to ease the tension of the last few days and try to move on.

He was not good when it came to expressing his feelings. I suppose that was the way he had been raised. After all, *boys do not cry*. Being emotional was considered a sign of weakness, an intrinsically feminine trait, and as such, frowned upon. Still, I could feel his love for me was pure and genuine and that the few times he told me *I love you*, he really meant it.

The calm after the storm did not last long.

His family still disapproved of our relationship, not only because I was a Christian, but also because we were not married before God.

My parents also shared similar concerns. Marrying a Muslim man was not exactly what they had wished for their beloved daughter when she left home at the tender age of eighteen to embark on a new adventure and pursue a degree at a prestigious British university. *All our sacrifices have gone down the drain*, they thought. But they also knew how stubborn and strong-minded their daughter was and that nothing they could say or do would stop her from doing what she wanted. So, after meeting him and seeing how caring he was, they were gradually resigned to the idea that their son-in-law would not join them for the midnight mass on Christmas Eve, eat *cotechino*[1] at New Year's or drink *prosecco* at the family gatherings.

Then the summer came, and with that, the end of our courses. It was time to make big decisions. Time to go back to the real world.

Would I ever find a journalist job? Where would I end up? Will Tahir's family ever accept me? Will he find a job here in the UK? I kept wondering, while Tahir had fears of his own.

Will I get a qualified job in the UK with my English level? Will I get a job anywhere? Will my family ever accept Sofia? Is my family right? Am I taking a wrong path by choosing a Christian? Will she ever convert?

We parted ways on a warm Sunday afternoon. It was the end of the summer break. I was still busy with my final project, which was aimed at investigating the main reasons for binge drinking in British society.

I had attended his graduation ceremony a few weeks before. I stood there among the crowd, like a proud wife, as he walked up the stage in his navy-blue graduation gown, handsome as ever, wondering what the future would hold for us.

He was looking forward to seeing his family again. To see his mother

---

[1] Italian pork sausage traditionally eaten with lentils on New Year's Eve.

who, as a loyal son, he felt responsible for since his father had passed away when he was only fourteen, and to see his siblings, nieces, and nephews, cousins, aunties, and uncles, all of whom were an essential part of his daily life before he had driven to Abu Dhabi and set on an eight-hour flight journey to the UK.

As we said goodbye on the platform, just minutes before he would catch a train to Manchester Airport, I knew that could have been the last time I saw him, but I tried all my best to push that thought out of my head.

"You take care," I uttered, fighting hard to hide the mix of emotions taking control of my mind. "You'd better come back soon if you don't want me to chase you across the desert on a camel!" I teased him defiantly. "No matter how long it may take, I *will* find you."

"*Insha'Allah*[2]," he replied, and off he went.

---

[2] "God willing."

CHAPTER TWO

You see it clearly when you feel the sun warming up your cheeks on a hot summer day. Those gorgeous yet rare days when the sky is cobalt blue and not a single cloud can be spotted on the horizon, and you wake up at dawn as the sunlight filters through the blinds. Those perfect moments when you feel like a tiny dot in the order of the universe, yet part of a bigger plan, as if your life and those of the billions of fellow human beings surrounding you were all intertwined … how calm and peaceful you feel when you look at the world that way.

Of course, I was sad about Tahir's departure, but I tried to keep as busy as I could not to overthink. After all, I was just about to complete the final year of my academic studies, which would hopefully lead me to a new, exciting start in my life. There was no time to waste, so I rolled up my sleeves, worked day and night, and handed in my project two weeks early. Once my thesis was out of the way, I focused on job hunting.

I had secured a two-week unpaid traineeship as a court reporter at the *Yorkshire Evening Post*, but I was still unsure where to go from there. I sent out CVs at random whenever a role that required fluency in one or more European languages was required.

Only a few days later, I received a response from a small London-based b2b publisher that was looking for an entry-level reporter to cover the IT industry in the Iberian markets.

How ironic was that! I was not exactly a techie, quite the opposite. I would have gladly swapped my HP Pavilion for a writing machine and often dreamt of living on a remote island with no Internet access.

But after a phone interview with the company director, a friendly chap who sounded eager to have me on board as soon as possible, I felt that was the chance I had been waiting for. A couple of hours later, I had already formally accepted their offer in writing, given notice to my landlady that I would vacate the room in a week's time, and started packing my bags. I was heading down to London, the Big Smoke, to kick-start my journalism career. What an amazing and unpredictable ride life can be!

The job involved travelling abroad to attend conferences and other industry events, which was one of the perks I most enjoyed. I joined a team of two reporters and an editor, a former IT professional in his fifties, who always had a seraphic and reassuring smile on his face. They made me feel welcome from day one.

Every Friday after work, we would go down the local pub for a drink and some chit-chat. "I have not seen my boyfriend for two full months," I told them on one such occasion. "He is coming over to visit me next week. I am literally counting down the hours," I added, beaming. "I *bet* you are," my boss replied, winking at me.

Two full moons without even seeing his face, as the Internet connection was weak in the area where he lived, and Skype did not work. He would call me every few days using a prepaid international calling card, but the rates were so high that we could only speak for a few minutes until the line would drop.

After returning home, he had faced lots of questions, particularly from the family elders, who tried to persuade him to end our relationship and marry a cousin instead, like most of his siblings had done.

However, after a few restless nights, when he would toss and turn in his bed asking God for guidance, one morning he woke up at dawn to the sound of the *adhan*[3], washed himself, and performed the *Fajr*[4] prayer. He went downstairs and greeted his mum, who was sitting on the beautifully embroidered Persian carpet adorning the living room, and tucked into the traditional breakfast she had prepared for him: Omani flatbread served with eggs, honey, and cream cheese, washed down with several cups of hot and sickeningly sweet *karak*[5] tea.

---

[3] The Muslim call to prayer.

[4] The third of the five prayers performed daily by practising Muslims.

[5] A blend of strong black tea, milk, sugar, and spices, typically cardamom.

After breakfast, he went to the mosque. He felt the urge to talk to someone about the dilemma that was tearing him apart, someone who was not emotionally involved in the matter, as he and his family were.

The local imam was a kind, wise man who was respected by the entire community. He listened to him carefully without ever interrupting him. When Tahir had finished sharing his story and he felt there was nothing else to add, the imam looked at him straight into the eyes and told him: "In Islam you are allowed to marry a Christian, provided she respects your religion. But you should marry her as soon as possible, not to be tempted and go astray."

Suddenly, it felt like a huge cloud had lifted, and a deep sense of relief pervaded his soul. *After we get married, my family will accept her, Insha'Allah. Just be patient. It is just a matter of time*, he told himself.

Now that he felt more comfortable with his decision, it was time to turn his attention to other pressing issues, like finding a job.

He had contacted his former employer, a multinational oilfield services company, hoping that he could get relocated to their Aberdeen office. However, they offered him an onshore drilling position in Mumbai, which he promptly accepted.

Now I am officially in a long-distance relationship, I thought, when he broke the news. I was upset, but at least he had managed to convince his family that he was serious about our relationship, and that was an achievement in itself. At that point, I felt nothing or nobody could have ever got in our way. We were too strong together.

Or so I thought.

I was holding a massive heart-shaped foil balloon as I waited for him at the Heathrow Airport arrival hall. "You have not changed a bit," I told him as he wrapped me in a tight embrace, the balloon going up in the air.

"You didn't either. Always so beautiful," he said, making me blush.

We spent the following few days making up for all the time we had been apart, telling each other all the things that can only be said face to face, locking eyes over endless cups of sugary Moroccan mint tea and baklavas.

Once, I even took him with me to work and introduced him to my colleagues-turned-friends. I showed him around Edgware Road, the North West London district sometimes called Little Cairo for its ubiquitous Arabic restaurants, cafés, and bars.

It was so great to finally be together again, waking up in the same bed in the immaculate single room that I had rented from a straightforward Japanese lady, who had climbed up the corporate ladder and owned a beautiful five-bedroom house on a leafy residential street in the suburban town of Uxbridge, in West London.

I adored the cross expression he had on his face while he was sound asleep, like a kid who was upset because his mum had not allowed him to have a second slice of cake. Years later, I would notice the same expression on our daughter's face, a constant reminder of our time together.

I could feel the warmth of our bodies desperately looking for each other, as the first rays of sunshine streamed through the windows, permeated by a feeling of safety and contentment while he pressed my chest against his and held me in a tight embrace.

But the week went fast, and when I saw him disappear through the security gates on his way to India, as I waved him goodbye from a distance, I could not hold back the tears.

∞

For the following eight months, our interactions consisted of bittersweet Skype video calls, whenever the fast pace of his oilfield job and the five-and-a-half-hour time difference would allow.

During the calls, we would share details of our daily lives. I would tell him about my work and also talk about more trivial things, like my culinary experiments. He was surprised at how unbelievably hot Indian food was, compared to the fragrantly spiced biryanis that the Sri Lankan maid who worked for his family back home used to make.

We would laugh, tease each other, hug, and kiss through the computer screen, and finally end the call with promises of unconditional and everlasting love, impatiently waiting for the moment we would finally be reunited once and for all.

That moment finally came, although it was not exactly as I had imagined it.

I was growing increasingly impatient and tired of all that longing that seemed to lead nowhere. I felt as if I had put my life on hold to wait for my Arabian prince, but at that point, I had started to doubt whether he would ever come back.

What if he didn't? What would I do about the years I had wasted chasing an impossible dream? All those sleepless nights holding onto memories of our brief time together.

It was time to make a painful yet rational choice and close this chapter for good.

One day, during one of our Skype video calls, I told him that, as much as I loved him, I could not see a future for us. That I had always wanted to settle down in England and progress in my journalism career here and that, unless he could join me as we had initially agreed, our relationship could not go any further. I was struggling to articulate those harsh words which had no place in my heart, yearning as it was day and night for his return.

We started fighting, as he tried to convince me to give him more time.

But that was me. I was not made for long-distance relationships, never had been. The intensity of the feelings I had for him meant that being so far away from the object of my love, unable to hold him in my arms, play with his hair, touch his skin whenever I desired, was too much of a burden. So, when he begged me to be patient and wait for some opportunity to come up, I did not budge.

"Did you forget the song, *baby*?" he pleaded, his voice husky from all the shouting. "*Wherever you go, whatever you do ... I will be right here waiting for you[6],*" he sang to me, stressing each word in a desperate attempt to release all the anger and sadness that had suddenly gripped his heart.

How many times had I listened to that song, as if the pure sound of it would make him materialise in front of my eyes?

"You take care," I replied, as the tears started rolling down my cheeks.

I was feeling dizzy, his words echoing in my head. *Did you forget the song? What about our promises? Please be patient! Insha'Allah, it will be fine.*

---

[6] "Right Here Waiting," by American singer and songwriter Richard Marx, released June 29, 1989.

When I woke up the following morning, I felt as if everything had been just a bad dream, but I was still too shaken to make sense of it. I preferred focusing on the busy workday that lay ahead of me and postpone any other thoughts, when I would be able to analyse the situation with a clear mind.

But what was there to analyse? Love is what it is ... either you fully embrace it and prepare yourself for the craziest ride of your life, or you don't and run away from it, I was telling myself as I was about to get into the shower.

Just then, the phone rang. It was Tahir informing me that he had just handed in his resignation letter and would be boarding a one-way flight to London the following morning.

I was trying to say something reasonable, like *you should not have done that,* or scold him for his impulsiveness, but all I could do was scream loud with excitement. "Can't wait to see you!" I said, my heart bursting with happiness.

CHAPTER THREE

When I opened the door and finally saw him in front of me, my enthusiasm quickly turned into a feeling of guilt. I felt selfish for having forced him to decide between his career and me, when I had been unwilling to do the same.

It was early 2008, and the financial crisis that had hit the global markets hard, had just started taking its toll on the oil and gas industry, with companies slashing thousands of jobs worldwide, including their Scottish offshore operations, and the most experienced employees being relocated to more profitable locations.

Finding work in that sector was out of the question, so he started looking for any other job where he could apply some of the skills and qualifications he had gained through his previous roles. But after months spent writing covering letters and fine-tuning CVs, walking up and down the streets of London and popping into every shop with a vacancy sign in its window; after landing a few interviews that would come to nothing, in an endless cycle of hope and disappointment, we had to face up to reality. He took up a temp job as a kitchen porter while we planned the next steps and made some alternative plans.

But that was not enough to ease his sense of frustration, exacerbated by the awareness that he had failed to comply with the social, cultural, and religious norms he had adhered to his whole life.

He had been raised with the idea that a man's value is defined by his ability to financially provide for his family and offer them protection and security. He was supposed to be the breadwinner, the head of the household, and the ultimate decision maker. Being jobless and forced to depend on your wife's salary to get by was considered particularly shameful and humiliating. An overwhelming sense of failure was gradually eroding his confidence, turning him into a lethargic and melancholic being.

"We must get married," he told me one night, as we sipped fresh mint tea, sitting on the carpet of the small bedroom that had become our safe haven.

I looked at him a little puzzled, but he continued unmoved. "We must do things properly, according to Islam. This is why all this is happening. Because we have not followed the correct steps."

Then, as he placed the cup back on the tray, he added, "We cannot continue to live together without being married in front of Allah. We should have the *nikah*[7], as soon as possible."

The pangs of guilt for living under the same roof without being man and wife kept him awake at night, piercing through his lungs and forcing him to hold his breath longer than required. He felt as if he had betrayed his God, his family, and himself. As if all the principles he had been taught since he was a little boy—and had fiercely defended throughout his youth—had been shattered into sharp, meaningless fragments cutting through his heart and tearing it apart.

I smiled at him and stroked his curly hair. *How much can one give up for love without losing himself?* I thought. "Don't worry, *habibi*. We will do the *nikah*[7]. Let's look for someone who can perform it for us," I said, trying to sound reassuring.

Just a few days later, on a cold bright Sunday morning at the beginning of December, we tied the knot through a religious Islamic ceremony in the home of a Pakistani imam whom Tahir had met at the local mosque. He had agreed to perform the ritual in return for a small offering to support the mosque's charity work.

I wore a silk emerald headscarf that was fully covering my neck and chest and I was made to repeat some words in Arabic which I had no clue about.

But I did not care. All that mattered was that getting married had put his torment to rest.

---

[7] Islamic marriage contract, or vows.

From that moment, we were husband and wife—at least in Islam—and everybody, including his family, had to acknowledge that.

∞

Maybe he was right, because a few days after the wedding, I received an offer for a subediting role in Dubai, where we had gone to escape the long British winter over the Christmas period.

It was the perfect honeymoon destination. I was dazed by the lights of the rapidly evolving city that never seemed to sleep. Dubai: City of Gold, a mirage in the desert, so often branded artificial and soulless by those who seemed envious of its richness and bold ambitions.

There is only one thing in the world worse than being talked about, and that is not being talked about, said Oscar Wilde.

Dubai—with its glamorous lifestyle, sky-high towers, gigantic shopping malls, and flashy sports cars clashing with the humble residences accommodating the thousands of migrant labourers who, through their strenuous work, turned the city's unquenchable appetite for dreams into reality—was neither perfect nor exempt from criticism, but precisely because of that, it was all but artificial. Indeed, its residents, who, despite the bad publicity, kept pouring in from all around the world in search of a better chance for themselves or their families, were what made Dubai truly authentic with all its flaws and imperfections. Dubai was like a woman—full of contradictions and hard to understand in the eyes of a man, but still ready to be loved.

After five wonderful days wandering around the narrow alleyways of Deira Old Souk, embarking on a few shopping sprees to Dubai Mall and Mall of the Emirates, strolling along the waterfront at Dubai Marina Walk, and scoffing down large platters of chicken *mandi*[8] washed down by cups of sugary karak tea, at the traditional mandi restaurants scattered around the city, we concluded that Dubai was the place for us.

---

[8] Traditional Yemeni dish consisting of meat and rice with a special blend of spices.

It was the best of both worlds, a city where East and West coexisted in harmony, where we could finally be ourselves and make our dreams come true.

Yes, we could find good jobs there and, one day, we would be able to buy a five-bedroom villa overlooking the sea on Jumeirah Beach Road, where the city's rich and powerful lived.

We would raise our children there and even set up our own business. Maybe we could open an Italian restaurant? Or a coffee shop? Or some kind of import-export business? After all, everything is possible in Dubai, isn't it?

Upon our return to London, I handed in my notice at work, and started making preparations for our move.

There are things that do not seem to make sense, feelings that cannot be defined, relationships that cannot be filed under any name. Questions that have no right or wrong answer, but that does not make them less real. They are still there, with all their beautiful contradictions. Some feel reassuring, familiar, reliable, like a book you read a thousand times, but which every time takes on new meanings that had passed unnoticed. Others take you aback and push you to get out of your comfort zone. They break walls that you did not even know existed and challenge all your assumptions. They surprise you like an unexpected gift that you cannot wait to unwrap, even though you are fully aware that, as perfect as it looks, you might not like what is inside the box. But that is what makes them so unique. Because they remind you that ahead lie a thousand possibilities, so long as you are brave enough to seize them.

This is how I felt as I packed my things into a dozen boxes ready to be shipped to Dubai and took a final look at the room that had been the centre of our life for the previous twelve months.

With the move underway, it was time to focus on our wedding celebrations. We still had to tell our entire families about our religious ceremony, but now that we were about to start a new life in the Gulf, it made sense to make our union public and official.

We had decided we would have a proper Omani wedding celebration at an exclusive resort in Muscat. I was thrilled at the idea of living a fairy tale among our friends and relatives, parading in my white wedding gown, which I had bought a few weeks earlier for 500 dollars during a work trip to New York. I would be next to my Arabian prince, who would wear a turban and a white *dishdasha*[9] adorned with the *khanjar*, the traditional Omani dagger still worn by Omani men on ceremonial occasions.

However, news of my wedding taking place in a country as remote as Oman, rather than in my hometown in Italy, did not go down well with my family.

"These kids nowadays … they always come up with such silly ideas," a relative said when I announced that, not only had I married a Muslim, but also that we would celebrate the wedding in my husband's city.

"Oman?!? That is so far! Why did you not do it like your sister who got married in Rome, in a *church*?" another echoed him, stressing the word *church* to get her message across.

"It was *my* idea," I promptly replied.

I have been away for too long to feel any connection to my birthplace. Also, I wanted to do something different. It is my special day after all and I wanted my guests to live a "One Thousand and One Nights" *kind of experience, to encourage them to discover my husband's culture and fall in love with it, as much as I did with him.*

I wish I could have said all of that, but I didn't. I was at a loss for words after all my excitement had been killed by such insensitive remarks. I simply said: "If you can come, I would very much appreciate it. But if you can't, I do understand."

Many of my friends had a similar reaction. None of them attended the celebrations, despite me offering to take care of the accommodation costs.

In the end, my guests consisted of only eight people: my parents; my sister and brother-in-law; and three of my best friends—two girls, one Hungarian and the other German, and a French guy who was accompanied by his fiancée.

The other one hundred attendees all belonged to Tahir's extended family, except for some neighbours and former colleagues.

[9] Long, usually white robe traditionally worn by men in the Middle East.

Nevertheless, I was glowing. I was finally able to share my happiness with the rest of the world. *This is the man I love and nothing you could say or do will take him away from me*, I felt like screaming at the top of my lungs. Everybody would now acknowledge our married status and I knew that, for him, the blessing of his community was far more important than it was for me.

I was a city girl raised in a fairly individualistic society where, as much as family ties are still relatively strong and can influence your thinking, in the end people tend to make independent choices and follow their own path, even if this may not conform to conventional social norms.

But he was born in a small village in a tribal society where an individual existed only as a member of his family clan. You could be a son or a daughter, a mother or a father, a wife or a husband, but what your predecessors had done in their lives, whether they were good or morally corrupt, could still dictate your fate and that of your descendants. And that was a very heavy burden to carry, which not even a love that did not know any boundaries could alleviate.

Now he felt validated and relieved as he prepared to embark on an exciting life journey with his foreign bride for whom he had fought against everybody, and even upset one of his aunts who had planned to marry off her daughter to him.

The party was a great success. The women danced and sang for the first two hours, all dolled up in their sophisticated ball gowns, dramatic make-up, and backcombed hairstyles.

As I walked down the party hall accompanied by my father—breaking local wedding etiquette—I could feel all eyes fixed on me. But my mind was focused only on the moment I would see my husband enter the hall and walk towards me. I ignored some disapproving stares and reached the stage, where I sat on the throne specially reserved for the newlyweds.

Then Tahir came, followed by his brothers, a few minutes after the women had covered up, hiding their colourful dresses and attractive shapes behind their black *abayas*[10], and had returned to their tables, as dancing in front of unrelated men was frowned upon.

---

[10] Loose (traditionally black) over-garment worn by some Muslim women.

How handsome he is! His mannerism, the way he carries himself, that angelic smile on his face. His soul is too pure to be just an ordinary human, I thought.

As we exchanged rings, my heart was swollen with pride.

A few well-wishers came up on the stage to congratulate us, then we took photos with our families and cut the cake.

As we danced to *I Will Always Be Right There*[11], once again breaking with tradition, I looked straight into his eyes which were as bright as ever.

"I love you," was all I could say, but an entire world was encased in those three words, waiting to come out and run wild. *I want you, I am proud of who you are, and I am not going to change you*, I wanted to say, but years down the line, I realised that this was easier said than done.

Can you truly accept someone as he is, even if who he is clashes with all the principles you have been standing by, way before you even knew of his existence? How far can one go before losing themselves?

---

[11] Song by Canadian singer and songwriter Bryan Adams, released on the album *18 till I Die* (1996).

CHAPTER FOUR

The move did not go to plan.

A few weeks into my new job, I concluded it was not for me. I missed the thrill of my previous reporting role, the adrenaline rush I would get every time one of my scoops went to press, and the satisfying sense of accomplishment that would follow. I could not see myself spending my days proofing articles written by someone else, my contribution to a story limited to the selection of a suitable headline and sub-heading, or rewriting press releases and uploading them onto a website.

No, I needed more than that.

Money was not a strong enough driver for me, although I had yet to meet someone who had chosen to become a journalist driven by financial considerations. They could have possibly been encouraged by the egotistic pleasure of seeing their name printed at the top of an article and being publicly recognised for their work. After all, there might be a certain degree of narcissism in the urge to share your own interpretation of reality with the rest of the world. But who is exempt from narcissism in a society where appearance and social media exposure are our bread and butter?

We flew back to the UK with mixed feelings. I did not really want to leave. I had been settling in well in Dubai. I was just unhappy with my job, but at that stage, I was not sure how long it would take to find another opportunity and I could not live there without an employment visa.

Tahir took that time as an opportunity to reorient his career. He signed up for a master's degree course in resource management at a prestigious university in Wales, where I would give Italian classes and work as a freelance translator to make ends meet.

We had rented a room in a house share in a picturesque village in The Vale of Glamorgan, but a few months after we had moved in, our landlord, who also lived at the same address, suddenly decided that letting out the only spare room had not been a good idea. The house was too small not to bump into each other every single day or to accommodate unexpected visitors, so, one night, without giving us any notice or giving us back our deposit, he informed us that we had to vacate the room the following day. We tried to make him come to his senses and pleaded with him to give us a few days to find another place. But once we saw that our presence was unwelcome, we decided not to insist further, packed our bags, and left without anywhere to go.

We were just about to check into a hotel in the centre of Cardiff while we looked for another room to rent, when we came across a shop window ad for student rooms. We called up the number provided and, a few hours later, we had become the new and only tenants of a nine-bedroom terraced house, whose Southeast Asian owner was more than happy to rent to us at a modest price while he waited for the next intake of students who were due to start their courses the following academic term.

Having such a big house all to ourselves was a little scary at first. Not only because it was just a few steps away from the city's main cemetery, but also because any sound reverberated through the empty rooms and was amplified over the three floors.

Still, we soon got used to it and even started imagining the day a house as big as that one would be ours. Although, in our dreams, the place would not be as quiet and empty. There would be screaming children running around, chasing each other, and filling the space with heart-warming laughter and life.

Something had changed inside of me since my first visit to Dubai. It was as if a part of me was still there. They call it *Mal d'Afrique*, that feeling of longing and nostalgia experienced by those who have travelled to Africa and feel an uncontrollable urge to go back.

But it was the Middle East I was longing for. My entire body and soul ached for places and faces too familiar to forget yet too foreign to call home, finding temporary solace in music, cinema, and literature which evoked those sceneries so dear to my heart.

"We must go back," I would often tell Tahir.

The year went fast, and when summer arrived, he had obtained his master's and secured a traineeship at a research-oriented university in Abu Dhabi. We thought that could be our chance to move back to the region and finally start building our life there.

Without thinking twice, I started applying for journalism positions in the UAE, until, a few weeks later, I received an offer to work as an editor on a business-to-business magazine at one of the largest publishing houses in the Middle East. I closed my eyes and accepted the offer. *This time it will be different*, an inner voice kept telling me.

That voice was right. This time things were indeed different. Everything about my new job was great: the location in the heart of Dubai's trendy media district; my team, a diverse group of talented and energetic professionals from all over the world, who performed their roles with passion and dedication; and the positive, creative vibes circulating throughout the office.

The only downside was that with Tahir in Abu Dhabi, we would be in two different cities, but 150 kilometres was no big deal for a couple who had overcome the challenges of a long-distance intercultural relationship.

We rented a one-bedroom flat in Discovery Gardens, a low-key residential development between Jebel Ali Village and Ibn Battuta Mall, a large shopping centre named after Moroccan Berber explorer Ibn Battuta, its design inspired by some of the countries he had visited. It was a convenient location, we thought, close to the motorway exit which would take Tahir to Abu Dhabi, and just a fifteen-minute drive to my office in Dubai Media City.

But at the end of Tahir's traineeship, the prospect of a permanent position became increasingly unlikely. Most Gulf countries were taking steps to prioritise the employment of their own citizens under a comprehensive localisation scheme aimed at reducing unemployment among Gulf nationals in both the public and private sectors. This presented us with yet another challenge.

An opportunity soon came, however, even though it was not the type of opportunity I had hoped for.

"My former employer wants me back," Tahir announced triumphantly as I was about to bite into my first slice of Margherita pizza at our favourite Italian restaurant on the Dubai Marina promenade.

"Great!" I replied, excited. "Would you still be working on the rig?" I asked, with some degree of trepidation.

"Yes. I will work on a six-three rotation," he explained, adding, after noticing my puzzled face: "I will be six weeks in the field, and three weeks off."

"*Six weeks in the field?* Wow ... where are you going to be based? Dubai? Sharjah? Abu Dhabi?"

"Not exactly. The job is in Oman," he said matter-of-factly.

"*Oman?*" I echoed, hoping I had not heard him properly.

"Yes. They want me to start next week," he whispered, in a vain attempt to ease the pain that those words inflicted.

I was not really sure what to say. It was a bombshell I was not prepared for, just when we were starting to feel settled in our new home and excited about our new life, and were even considering starting a family. I wanted to urge him not to go, ask him to be patient, tell him that it was only a matter of time before he would find something better in Dubai, that we did not need the money because my salary was enough for both of us. But then, I suddenly remembered how his eyes, those eyes I loved looking into so much, had lost their sparkle after he had put his career on hold to follow me halfway across the world. I also remembered how they had lit up once again the day he had been offered the traineeship. How thrilled he was at the prospect of moving back to the Middle East, to be closer to his people, to feel at ease among familiar sights and sounds.

No, I could not be so selfish. What if nothing better would come up? What if he would blame me for that later on? What if the resentment over giving up the job led to repercussions on our relationship? Being away from each other after getting used to spending most of our time together would have been really tough, of course, but we had proved to the entire world that our love was stronger than everything.

In a matter of days, he was gone, and I found myself alone in a city that I was still trying to figure out, whose vast array of smells, sights, and sounds was still dauntingly unknown. I was used to the reassuring predictability of England, where in every place, from a tiny village to the largest city, one can spot familiar sights, from a high-street retailer, such as Boots or Marks & Spencer, to a local post office, pub, or corner shop.

I tried to keep myself busy with work, hanging out with my colleagues, venturing into the old souk, shopping at one of the city's gigantic malls, jogging at sunset along Jumeirah corniche.

But time never seemed to pass quickly enough. Not at a pace half as fast as that of the operations on the rig which would run non-stop day and night, allowing us to talk for no more than five minutes every twenty-four hours.

Still, hearing Tahir's tired voice on the other end of the line was the only antidote for my aching soul.

I would keep telling myself that this was a temporary arrangement, that soon we would be reunited forever, but as the time went by, it became harder for him to leave the job without a valid alternative. We were getting stuck in a routine made of goodbyes and welcome backs, of days apart lasting an eternity, and those together gone in the blink of an eye.

During the three weeks he was off work, Tahir would try to make up for the lost memories, taking me on camping trips to the desert, eating out in our favourite restaurants, catching up on the latest Bollywood releases, and just enjoying each other's company.

There were days, though, when he would be too tired to leave the sofa as his body struggled to recover from the sleepless nights in the field, the dust that would get into his lungs, the stress of working under high pressure in an extreme environment. I was worried that his job was affecting his health, but he would reassure me that he could manage himself and that he would quit as soon as he had made enough money to secure our future.

A few months into the job, he decided to take out a loan to buy our first car, which would allow him to commute more easily between Muscat and Dubai, a six-hour drive interspersed with sandy dunes, camels, date palms, rocky mountains, traditional villages, checkpoints, petrol stations, and people selling rugs, fruit, or *bakhoor*[12] at the side of the road.

With the rest of the loan, he bought land in Muscat on which he planned to build a mixed-use development comprising flats as well as retail outlets. If everything went to plan, in a couple of years he would be able to repay the loan and make a return on his investment.

Everything seemed to be falling into place for us. After a few failed attempts, we had recently obtained a non-objection certificate from the Omani government, which we needed for our marriage to be legally recognised in Oman. I had been promoted to a more senior role, overseeing two new b2b titles, which meant more responsibilities and longer working hours, but also a bigger salary.

"This is the right time," I told him confidently on a lazy Saturday afternoon in our Dubai home. It was 3 p.m. and we were still in bed, cuddling each other, daydreaming about our future, and passionately discussing global politics, voicing our disappointment with the direction the world was taking.

"Let's have a baby. If we want three, we should get started," I teased him.

"Yes, you are right. I wish we could have a mini Sofia who runs around the house and talks nonstop just like her mother," he shot back.

"I don't mind if our first child is a boy or a girl, as long as he is healthy … and looks just like you!" I laughed.

---

[12] Incense traditionally used on the Arabian Peninsula to fragrance the house, hair, and clothing.

CHAPTER FIVE

O ur wishes were fulfilled.

A few months later, on a visit to my family in Rome, I found out I was pregnant.

We had just returned from a one-week stay at a glamorous five-star resort in the Maldives, taking advantage of the abundance of all-inclusive last-minute deals aimed at boosting tourism during the monsoon season.

Despite the rain, we had an amazing time, making the most of our cosy bungalow with private access to the beach, snorkelling in the Indian Ocean, and savouring both local and international delicacies at the many Michelin-starred restaurants available in the resort.

I was shocked and saddened by the stark contrast between the poverty of the capital, Malé, and the luxury of the hotel developments on the other islands; between the bustle of a densely populated city and the quietness of the tourist resorts; between the simplicity of the local residents and the glamour of their affluent visitors. But then I thought that after all, tourism was a main source of income for the islanders. So I felt a little relieved at the thought that, by strolling along Maldives' immaculate beaches, diving into its blue lagoons, and admiring its spectacular coral reefs, I was somehow contributing to the local economy.

That was what I was thinking as I showed the photos we had taken during our holiday to my mum. "You look different," she immediately said, although she could not put the finger on what in my appearance had changed. "Have you dyed your hair? No, it is something to do with your face … it has a special glow," she asserted, like someone that had finally succeeded in solving a head-scratching mystery.

She may be right, I told myself, because not only did I look different, but I was feeling different too.

That night, I went to bed early, blaming the five-hour flight from Dubai for my drowsiness.

But then, I suddenly woke up at three in the morning and found it impossible to go back to sleep. I took out the pregnancy test hidden among the clothes still packed in my suitcase and went to the bathroom, determined to confirm my expectant status.

A few minutes later, I was sitting on the edge of the bathtub staring at the test's display which showed that the baby had been conceived three weeks before.

It is impossible to describe the explosive mix of emotions that shook my whole body as I read the results. I was overjoyed, frightened, and confused, to say the least. *Was this really happening?* They say, no matter how long you have been waiting for that moment, and how well informed you are about the subject, nothing will ever prepare you for motherhood, which in your mind and body starts well before you even get to know that tiny being growing inside of you that will become your own child.

Of course, the first person I broke the news to was Tahir. He was working on the rig that night so I knew he would be awake, even though he might not have the time to answer the phone.

The phone rang three times, but when I was about to hang up, I heard his croaky voice on the other end of the line.

"We made it, my love. I am pregnant!" I screamed, struggling to hold back the emotion.

"*Bismillah*[13]," Tahir replied, before adding with his usual prudent scepticism: "This is just the first step of the journey."

We could only exchange a few words, as he had to go back and monitor the operations.

Indeed, it was only the first step, but this tiny dot living inside of

---

[13] "In the name of Allah," a phrase often used by Muslims when they embark on a significant endeavour.

me had already managed to change me. I was not the same person who had entered the bathroom an hour before, my hands shaky as I waited for the test result with growing trepidation. Now I was a mother-to-be, although I still did not know exactly what that entailed.

Going back to sleep was out of the question, and so was waking up the rest of the household to share the news. I decided to write. Since I was a child, it had been my favourite way of letting out my emotions.

I wish you look like your father, with his lively eyes and long eyelashes.
I wish you will fill this void and replace it with joy.
I wish you are born free and healthy, because that's all that matters.
I wish I will be able to show you that life is beautiful.
I wish you will be able to teach me to love and be loved.
I wish you will fight for your rights and defend your ideas.
I wish you are not just a dream living inside me.

Once the news had spread across our entire families, who were as thrilled as we were, we agreed that it would make sense for me to spend the first few months of my pregnancy in Rome, since the idea of being completely alone in Dubai in my current state, when Tahir was in the field, did not particularly entice me.

I would take some unpaid time off work while I figured out what to do, and Tahir could still visit me when he was back from the field. But when I entered the fourth month of pregnancy and I felt reassured that everything was going smoothly, I decided to put an end to my self-imposed exile. It was time to go back to the "sandpit," as Dubai expats had labelled the place, to our cosy love nest which would soon be home to our new family.

Upon my return, I spent the first few days shopping for baby gear and decorating the nursery. By the time I was thirty weeks pregnant, I had splashed out on a wide range of so-called "baby essentials," most of which, as most first-time mothers soon realise, are anything but essential.

My twenty-week scan had confirmed our gut feeling—we were expecting a girl! We decided to call her Amal, which in Arabic means *hope*. I had fallen in love with the name after reading *Mornings in Jenin* by Susan Abulhawa. In her book, Amal is a strong and resilient girl who grows up in the Palestinian refugee camp in Jenin. She faces a lot of struggles in her life, but she never gives up.

That's how I imagined my daughter would be—a girl of strong and resolute character who would bring hope to the world from her very first day of life.

But just when the due date was approaching, Tahir broke some bad news to me which he had kept to himself for fear that it could somehow affect my pregnancy. His project in Oman, which he had been working on together with his brother, was not going well. He had lost a big chunk of money due to a dispute with a distant relative, who was supposed to pay them for the house they had been building for him but had later changed his mind and disagreed on the final price. They could have sued him in court, but they had an informal agreement rather than a legally binding contract, and anyway, that was not the way they did things over there. They would just talk to him and hopefully reach an understanding, but it would take time. Meanwhile, the project would be put on hold indefinitely.

I could not believe my ears. *Perfect timing!* I thought as I was trying to keep calm and come up with some sort of solution.

I had just gone back to work, but I was only offered a part-time contract. For now, it suited me, as reduced working hours meant I could have more time to attend hospital appointments and prenatal classes, take care of the house, and make some last-minute preparations for the baby's arrival. But having a baby in Dubai was an expensive affair, and our private health insurance was only partly covering maternity costs. And as much as Tahir was trying to sound reassuring, I could spot a worried frown on his face.

We were sitting in a busy coffee shop inside The Dubai Mall, drinking karak tea and watching over-enthusiastic shoppers strolling up and down Fashion Avenue, the mall's luxury designer fashion district and a shopaholic's paradise.

We certainly did not need a tenth of all that luxury to be happy. Neither did our soon-to-be-born baby.

I took Tahir's hand and pressed it tightly in mine. I needed to feel him as close to me as ever.

I knew he was averse to public displays of affection. That was just the way he had been brought up, and I respected that, but on that occasion, I broke those unwritten rules. I did not want to let any traditional customs repress my feelings and kill the spontaneity of a moment that would be lost for eternity.

"It's okay. We will be fine, Insha'Allah. We will try to save as much as we can and will pay off the loan little by little. Money comes and goes, after all. But we still have *us*. That's all that matters," I told him smiling, trying to break down the first bricks of the invisible wall he had just started erecting between us.

CHAPTER SIX

Amal was born on a beautiful spring day in early May at a private state-of-the-art hospital in Dubai Healthcare City, looking the spitting image of her father.

We had to resort to the help of our families to cover the hospital stay, but when we held that cute, chubby bundle of joy in our arms for the first time, we felt that no money in the world was worth as much as her sheer existence.

We had to stay in the hospital five days longer than planned, as Amal was placed under observation in the intensive care unit for suspected jaundice.

Tahir stayed by my side day and night. I had been so relieved when, as I lay on the cold operating table, nearly fainting from the effect of the anaesthetic, I felt his hand grabbing mine as if he meant to say: *Don't worry, I won't let you fall. Your guardian angel will watch over you.*

Watching his slim body curled up in the small sofa next to my hospital bed, I recalled our first encounter five years before. How much had changed since that random night.

We had fallen in love, got married, moved to another country, and now we were having our first baby, a baby that, as the gynaecologist who had carried out my 4D scan a few weeks before anticipated, had "quite a temper." The doctor had poked me in the belly to see if the baby responded to the pressure, but what he had not expected was that Amal would kick him back with all the strength a thirty-five-week foetus could have.

Yes, she was strong, in all possible ways, but the amount of joy she would bring to our life could have certainly not been anticipated.

It was like all the life that I felt rushing through my veins, and all the love and passion Tahir and I had for each other, had blended and materialised into a new being, one so unique and different from her own parents on so many levels, yet a perfect mirror of their best traits.

Indeed, from a very tender age, Amal seemed to be well aware of her mixed identity and very proud of it. She loved pizza as much as Mandi rice and Parmesan cheese as much as dates. She would shake her body like crazy as soon as she heard Arabic tunes, but she was equally fond of Italian pop songs. She was our Roman Bedouin girl and that was exactly what made her so special.

When we were finally able to leave the hospital, we received a surprise visit from Tahir's mum and siblings, who had travelled all the way from Muscat to pay their respects to the first-time parents and shower the newborn with their blessings.

After being confined to a hospital bed for five long days, I was keen to enjoy the intimacy of my own place with my new family. But to show his family my appreciation for their kind gesture and make them feel welcome, I told Tahir to invite them to stay a few days in our house so that they could spend some time with us and the baby. In the end, however, only two of his little sisters took up the invite, while the others politely declined.

According to Islamic tradition, a woman who has given birth is supposed to stay at home for the first forty days to recover from delivery, usually in her mother's home. Tahir's family knew that, as a non-Muslim, I would have not followed all the traditional birth rituals that Omani women adhered to, including shaving the newborn's hair on her seventh day of life, or eating special foods to increase breast milk supply.

However, his mum, a simple, soft-spoken woman who had given birth to eleven healthy children, most of whom had come into the world in the privacy of her home, tried her best to share her post-birth knowledge and experience. She suggested that I should drink fenugreek tea, along with a special herbal concoction, every few hours, wrap the baby tightly, avoid giving her a dummy, and follow a few other instructions I have forgotten by now.

Years before, as the rebellious teenager I had been, I would have found her suggestions inopportune and intrusive. But I had grown up enough to realise that her intentions were good, that she genuinely cared for us, and only wanted to show her love for her new grandchild as best she could.

Her discreet attitude was far different from the snide remarks I had received from one of Tahir's aunties who, as she whispered excerpts from the Quran into Amal's ears, had promptly stressed that the baby, as the daughter of a Muslim, was herself Muslim by birth.

"You chose a Muslim name for her. She is indeed Muslim, and she will be raised according to Islam," she had stated, giving me a defiant and inquisitive look, as if she wanted to test how far she could go.

I did not reply. From the first moment Tahir and I had talked about starting a family, I knew that he would have wanted our children to learn about Islam and be raised as Muslims. And although I was not a particularly religious person myself, I could see how his faith had helped him feel more grounded and content and accept daily life struggles with serene resignation. For someone like myself, however, who strongly believed that one could get anything he wanted, provided he fought hard enough to achieve his goals, it was at times irritating. I could not understand how he could live like nothing could really affect him or undermine his certainties. How could he just shrug his shoulders, and mutter a *Let's see* or *What can I do?* every time I presented him with a problem? *No, I did not want to see. I just wanted to live as best as I could, possibly today and not at some point in the future.*

To me that sounded like an excuse not to take control of his life.

What can you do? You can do a lot actually … what about not being passive and taking some action, rather than waiting for things to happen? I would think, frustrated that he would not take my concerns as seriously as I expected. His lack of initiative would often put me off. I would have liked him to be more proactive and assertive, to fight against any injustice and above all, to fight to save our relationship and our family.

∞

From his perspective, he was doing all of that, although his efforts were not going in the same direction as mine.

He went back to work after spending the first month of Amal's life together with me, gradually mastering the art of nappy changing and even turning it into an enjoyable experience, taking turns feeding, burping, and cuddling the baby at night, sometimes even taking her on a 4 a.m. drive along Jumeirah Beach Road, in a desperate attempt at getting her to sleep, after all other possible and impossible tricks mentioned in the parenting books I had avidly consumed during my pregnancy had failed to work.

As soon as the door closed behind him, and I was left on my own with a one-month-old baby I had just begun to know, I felt completely lost. *What am I going to do now? What if she cries so hard that the neighbours think someone is stabbing her to death and report me to the police? And even if they do not call the police, will everybody think I am a terrible mother?*

Everybody told me that nothing in life brings as much happiness as motherhood. *Then, why do I just feel constantly exhausted and frightened?*

The emotional and physical rollercoaster that becoming a mother leads to was starting to take a toll on me.

It's like a part of your old self is lost, never to come back, while a new you, who you don't really know, takes over. It takes time and lots of patience to get to know that new person, but as you go along, she becomes more and more familiar, just like your new baby.

I would spend my days strolling up and down Ibn Battuta Mall, watching Amal as she lay sound asleep in her pushchair. She seemed able to doze off only when amid the endless babble of the multitude of eager shoppers that inundated the mall day in day out. That was also the only time of the day I could take a break from my parenting duties and unwind drinking cappuccino and watching the world go by, as I sat in one of the comfy armchairs of my favourite Starbucks, located right in the middle of the Persia Court. Sometimes, I would get together with other first-time mums, whom I had met at my prenatal classes, and their babies. I enjoyed spending time with them, as they shared the same fears and sense of isolation that having a baby in a foreign country, away from your family and friends, can often lead to.

We were all trying to support each other, sharing breastfeeding and sleeping tips and rewarding ourselves with a quick trip to Debenhams while the babies were asleep. More often than not though, I would just sit there alone, trying to catch up on the pile of books which lay on my bedside table since the baby was born; I was always too exhausted at night to get past the first page.

After a few hours, I would go back home, where, as soon as I crossed the doorstep, Amal would wake up, crying desperately. I would then try to comfort her and cuddle her as best as I could, holding her tight in my arms and whispering old Italian lullabies into her ear after feeding her.

Nobody had told me how painful breastfeeding could be. I was literally crying my eyes out the first times the nurse had woken me up in the middle of the night to bring me my ravenous baby from the ICU. Once, when Amal latched onto my breast, she started sucking so vigorously that I let out an ear-piercing shriek, which led the nurse to label her *baby vampire*.

However, over the following few weeks, things gradually settled. I was truly enjoying watching how she would rest her perfectly round little head on my chest after nursing her in the wooden rocking chair next to the bedroom window. I had decorated the room in shades of pastel colours during the last month of my pregnancy, hoping they would have a soothing effect on the baby.

Those were our special mother-and-daughter moments, bonding times I would not have given up for anything in the world. During those moments, I would feel as if she were still in my womb, reassured and protected by the warmth of my body, slowly shaping into a distinct being with her own unique features and personality, yet still connected to the person from whom she had come. We were two people in one in those unforgettable moments, and I wished I could hold her like that forever. Though I knew that, as my favourite poem went, *Your children are not your children. They are the sons and daughters of Life's longing for itself* [4]. I was fully aware that, no matter what I did to keep

---

[4] From "On Children" published in *The Prophet* (1923) by Lebanon-born poet and author Kahlil Gibran.

her close to me, one day not so far off she would leave the nest and just fly away. And, as challenging as that could have been, my primary role was to provide her with wings to fly, roots to hold her, and memories to cherish.

And that was what I was determined to do.

I was also fairly sure that I would not be like one of these so-called "helicopter mums" who do not let their children live their own experiences in a vain attempt to protect them from any harm, just like traditional Italian parents tend to do. No, I would be different.

I had experienced first-hand the emotional damage that an overprotective and anxious parent can cause to children which, when combined with a tendency to interfere in every aspect of their lives and be excessively critical of any initiative they dare take that does not fit within the rigid boundaries imposed by the parent, often creates a deep sense of insecurity and inadequacy in young minds. That's not what I wanted for my daughter. I wanted to love her in a more selfless and healthier way. I wanted her to grow strong and independent, to prepare her for the ruthlessness of life. I wanted her to run wild and free, to travel far and wide, to find her way and get lost, confident that, no matter how far she would go or how many times she would feel disoriented, she would never forget the way back home.

But more than anything, I wanted to show her what it meant to love someone so much that you were not afraid of letting them go.

CHAPTER SEVEN

Tahir finally came back. It was the start of the *Eid al-Fitr* holidays, which mark the end of the holy month of Ramadan, and we decided to visit his family in Muscat, as every single one of them was eager to meet the baby.

We left Dubai at dawn, hoping to avoid the traffic of people travelling to the Oman border for the so-called *visa run*, which would allow them to extend their UAE stay, locals visiting their relatives in the villages, expats enjoying a relaxing getaway at one of the many luxury resorts scattered across the desert.

Despite our efforts, however, we got stuck for a couple of hours at the UAE border, waiting in a long queue to get my passport stamped.

The fact that Tahir was married to a non-*Khaleeji*, as the inhabitants of the Arabian Peninsula call themselves, and even worse, to a Westerner, always aroused suspicion among government officials. People did not seem able to comprehend why a Gulf citizen would want to marry outside his race, especially someone who did not share his religion, language, and culture. How could traditional customs and family honour be preserved if one married a disbeliever? And what was the need to *marry* a Western girl, if you could just *have sex* with her? some of Tahir's friends had asked him when he announced that we had got married.

It was the same kind of prejudice I had come across among some of my own people, who wrongly assumed that I had married Tahir, the Arab sheikh, as they used to mock him, for money, as if our relationship could only be based on an opportunistic exchange.

The officer checked my passport thoroughly. "Is she your *maid*?" he asked abruptly in Arabic. "No, she is my *wife*," Tahir replied, composed, with his usual nonchalance.

The officer's expression suddenly changed. He must have felt he had crossed a line he should not have crossed and let us go without even checking the boot of the car for drugs or other illegal items, as was usually the case. "He thought you were my maid," Tahir explained handing me back my passport. I laughed.

I would normally let him do the talking in any situation that required interaction with public officials. I knew that would have saved us plenty of time and a headache. Plus, that was what everybody seemed to expect—that a man would talk in public on behalf of his wife. And as much as the control freak in me would find it hard to step back at times, I gradually accepted the idea that, in our household, he would be responsible for all practical and bureaucratic matters.

As we approached Muscat, I started spotting the white low-rise buildings lined up along the corniche overlooking the Gulf of Oman, which reminded me of Apulia, the southern Italian region where my father came from, and where I had spent so many carefree summers as a child, playing with my sister in the crystalline waters of the Ionian Sea.

We arrived early afternoon. Amal was sound asleep in her car seat, but when we parked, we found a large party of people waiting in front of the house to welcome us.

It was a Friday, the first day of the weekend in Gulf countries, and the day when all of Tahir's family would gather at his mum's to eat, chat, and pray together.

We were about to get out of the car when Tahir's mother took Amal out of the car seat, waking her up.

"*Masha'Allah!*[15]" she said, kissing and cuddling the baby, who stared at the unfamiliar face confused.

The men greeted each other in the traditional Bedouin way, touching their noses to one another, while the women kissed me and shook my hand.

---

[15] "What God has willed has happened."

We were ushered inside the house as the kids helped Tahir take our luggage out of the car.

We had stopped at a small confectionery on the way to buy *halwa*, a traditional jelly-like sweet flavoured with saffron, cardamom, nuts, and rosewater, so I presented the small gift to my mother-in-law, and she thanked me profusely. I found most Arabic sweets too sugary for my liking, but I knew she had a sweet tooth, so the treat would have been appreciated.

Tahir had joined the other men in the *majlis* through the side entrance of the house, where they would gather when unrelated male guests paid a visit. It was decorated with colourful cushions, Baroque wallpaper, and Persian carpets, and included an en suite bathroom where the men would perform their ablutions before each daily prayer. Canvases featuring quotes from the Quran in golden Arabic characters were hanging on the walls, along with a couple of landscape paintings.

As I watched Tahir chatting to his relatives before vanishing into the majlis, I noticed how his face had changed since we had crossed the Oman border, as if he could finally lift the mask he put on when he was away from home. I could see how at ease he was among his people, laughing and joking like I had rarely seen him doing in the previous months. It was as if he could only be truly and fully himself in his home country, within the four walls of his mother's house, where not only did he feel safe and comfortable but also valued and respected.

Realising that the person I loved more than anything in this world looked happier with *his* family than with *ours*, the one we had just started to build after overcoming many hurdles, was a truth too hard to swallow.

At first, I tried to ignore it. I could give up everything except us, that feeling of calm when he was around. He was on the other side of my universe, so different yet so alike, sometimes so far and other times so close.

It was true. Our worlds did not understand each other, but we did not even need to talk. He was my past, my present, and my future. My roots, my home, and my wings. And that's all that mattered.

So, I pretended not to see that we were drifting apart day after day. I began to ignore the hours he spent chatting with his friends and family back home, completely oblivious to what was going on around him. I was finding it hard to keep up with the ever-changing business ideas he would come up with every few days.

"We could open a pizzeria in Muscat, and then, with the returns, we could build a villa next to my mum's," he would tell me with an overenthusiastic tone, trying to win me over.

"We could do the same in Dubai," I would then reply. "You know I never wanted to settle down in Muscat," which was usually followed by a bitter silence.

We were slowly becoming aware that we wanted different things. He wanted to live a simple life in Muscat, building a house near his family, finding a steady government job that would give him long-term security, setting up a small side business with his brothers and uncles, spending his spare time watching and playing football with his friends, attending the Friday gatherings at his mum's and the other family engagements. Maybe, once he had enough of city life, he would move to a little village at the foot of the Hajar Mountains, living from the produce of his own garden.

But his world seemed too limited for an adventurous globetrotter like me for whom the world had no boundaries. I wanted to succeed in my journalism career, buy a nice house in Dubai, and travel far and wide with my husband and our children. I wanted us to make our own plans and take decisions as a family, without the need to involve our respective families in our projects, whether these entailed a holiday abroad or a new business.

I loved living in Dubai because it allowed us to do all of that. In Dubai, we could just get on with our lives, without what I saw as constant interferences from his people, whom we could still visit a couple of times a month. In Dubai, he could wear Western clothes rather than the Omani dishdasha, and I did not have to wear the veil just to avoid the gossip from some acquaintance we may have bumped into on a trip to Mutrah Souq. In Dubai, it was just me and him. What people might think did not matter.

But in Muscat, it was a different story. I felt as if every single thing I did or said would be constantly judged. Just as Tahir was lifting his mask at home, I would be putting one on and start playing a part which did not suit me in the slightest. I was to be the modest and reserved wife: that was the role imposed upon me by local customs. I needed to remember how to sit, how to eat, and how to behave not to offend local sensitivities. I was careful not to delve into parts of my identity that could have been considered too daring or over-the-top. I was not able to enjoy the time I would spend with his sisters, with whom I could easily communicate in English, because I was too focused on being the perfect wife and mother who would make Tahir proud and reassure him that he had made the right choice.

I was trying my best to fit in, yet I was always feeling like I was failing him and his family. I was finding it mentally and emotionally exhausting to follow all those unwritten rules, like remembering to say Masha'Allah every time someone complimented our baby to avoid attracting the evil eye.

It was nearly fifty degrees, and my clothes were sticking to my body from the sweat. I was desperate for a shower, but Tahir's sisters and sisters-in-law had put on a feast of scrumptious finger food, from meat and vegetable *sambousek* to salted cod and potato fritters, dates, fruit, and baklavas, served with *kahwa*, the traditional Omani coffee. I would always feel honoured and humbled by such a heart-warming display of hospitality.

I took a quick trip to the bathroom to freshen up and sat on the soft carpet at the centre of the living room specially reserved for the women of the house, which was covered with a thin plastic tablecloth to protect it from food stains.

The women served me first to show their respect towards a new guest. I waited for everybody else to get served and say Bismillah before starting to eat, making sure that my crossed legs would stay covered throughout the meal, hidden behind the long skirt I had worn for the occasion, and also that my headscarf would stay in place to avoid accidentally revealing any strand of hair.

When we finished eating, Tahir's mum signalled that they would all go to pray in the adjacent room.

She put Amal in my arms, who had become acquainted with her grandma's features and had peacefully lain on her lap until that moment. I started nursing her, covering my breast with my scarf, as the kids stared at the baby with a mix of curiosity and amazement.

When the women returned, they all started helping each other clear the carpet, taking away the dirty dishes and cups and brushing away any remaining crumbs.

Our conversations were limited to kind yet formal interactions, where we would enquire about each other's progress with work or study, or we would express mutual sympathy over the children's seasonal ailments.

Every time I visited, I would be introduced to a new member of the family, who was just born or was still in the making.

I was always careful not to cross that invisible line that separates the private matters of a household from the public sphere, and never discussed the kind of issues I would talk about with my girlfriends, including things like relationships, sex, and periods.

I was perfectly aware that these were taboo subjects in such a conservative culture, like it was sharing someone's marital problems, but because there were so many boundaries I dared not and could not cross, I was finding our exchanges shallow and superficial. It was so frustrating not to be able to get to the core of a person, to discover her most intimate desires, despite knowing her for many years. I felt as if I was missing out on a once-in-a-lifetime chance to get to know other women—some of them the same age as me—from a different culture, and get to know my own husband through them, but I did not want to cause any embarrassment to themselves and Tahir by asking the wrong questions. I would have liked to know if they were really happy, what kept them awake at night other than their children, their dreams, and their fears, whether they felt as overwhelmed by all the social norms they were expected to comply with as I was, whether they wished they would only have to be accountable to themselves and nobody else for their actions.

Tahir entered the room, interrupting the stream of thoughts running through my head. He just wanted to let me know that he would travel to a village just outside Muscat with the other men to visit a sick uncle and would come back late at night. I sighed. I was dreading the idea of spending another few hours at home with his female relatives, wearing a fake smile and squeezing my brain to come up with uncontroversial conversation topics.

But there was not much I could do about that. All the other men were going, and I did not want to come across as the foreign wife who bosses her husband around in the eyes of his family.

I just nodded my head and told him I would try to rest in the upstairs bedroom once I managed to get Amal to sleep.

The days were so slow for me on those visits.

The kids would be having fun, playing with each other, and showing off the brand-new dresses their parents had bought for them to celebrate Eid, as required by tradition. The women were busy all day chatting and cooking for hundreds of guests, while the men would prepare *shuwa*, a traditional Omani festive dish made by slaughtering a goat, wrapping the marinated meat in banana leaves, and then digging a hole in the ground where it would be slow-roasted for at least twenty-four hours.

But as much as I tried my best to feel part of their community, wearing the same loose brightly coloured dresses the women would wear on such occasions and trying to display the same degree of enthusiasm they shared, I could not avoid feeling out of place, an outsider who had imposed herself on a world that did not belong to her.

Tahir was probably thinking the same on those few occasions when we celebrated Christmas in Rome with my family. He would eat our festive food, after someone would make him notice, with a slightly irritating paternalistic tone, that they had intentionally served the mozzarella cheese and the prosciutto in two separate plates, so that he would not come into contact with any trace of pork.

After eating, however, he would often sit alone in a corner on the sofa, as we organised the religious ritual that we would perform every Christmas Eve just before midnight before exchanging presents.

We would line up in a queue singing Christmas worship songs, the person at the front holding a candle. We would then walk into every room of the house to bless it, and finally the youngest in the family would announce the birth of Jesus Christ, by placing the nativity figurine of infant Jesus back in his crib. Even after the procession was over, and we would be busy unwrapping the presents, Tahir would still look uncomfortable, playing with his phone and isolating himself from the rest of the family, as if he wished he were somewhere else.

I must admit that his lack of enthusiasm saddened me a little. I wished he had made a greater effort to adjust to some of our traditions— at least those that had no religious implication—as I felt I was trying to do by embracing parts of his culture. But there were times I would feel bad about thinking that. We were just two worlds apart, and that was nobody's fault.

Was I trying too hard to force something that was starting to affect our own happiness? Why couldn't we just accept that we would never become what we wanted the other to be?

Maybe he hoped I would change. Maybe he hoped his love could change me, curb my eccentric fashion style, the way I would get overexcited about the most trivial things, my uncontrollable laughing fits, which, more often than not, were triggered by the bittersweet irony of everyday situations, my spontaneous displays of affection, and any other traits which he considered embarrassing and unseemly for a married woman.

Maybe I, on the other hand, hoped I would always come first in his eyes: before his family and friends, before any job he could get, and even before his religion.

But the reality is that nobody can change his nature, nor his identity. Not even for love.

CHAPTER EIGHT

When we got back to Dubai, I was more resolute than ever to find a solution to all the pending issues that were making us feel unsettled in our lives.

Tahir was starting to get sick of his job—the twelve-hour shifts in sizzling temperatures, the long commute between Muscat and Dubai, the delays at the border, the stress of packing and unpacking bags every few weeks, feeling like he had no proper roots.

He slowly became obsessed with the idea of moving to Oman and building our future there. I would not even need to work if I did not want to. I could have a maid, a gardener, and even a driver there, he would tell me, hoping that the thought of these little luxuries would win me over. What he did not seem to understand was that I did not find any of those comforts appealing in the slightest. A good life to me meant a life lived to the full. Working with passion, travelling far and wide, filling the days with exciting activities. Doing as little as possible in the comfort of my own home was not exactly my idea of enjoyment. I craved adventure, dynamism, the thrill of the unknown.

He craved stability and security, and maybe that was why our goals diverged so much.

I had convinced him to sell the plot of land he bought in Muscat since the project had been stalled for nearly a year and, if we wanted to change our situation, we needed to pay off the loan as soon as possible. He eventually gave in and managed to recover part of the investment.

Amal had just turned one, and I had started to become more confident about my parenting skills, thanks in part to the help of my neighbour, who had eagerly agreed to babysit her a few hours a day. Her husband was working away, and she was tired of spending her days alone at home waiting for his return.

When I had first met her, she was sitting alone on a bench in the courtyard in the middle of our development, watching kids playing football and cycling around the buildings. She looked bored, but her eyes immediately brightened up when I sat next to her holding Amal in my arms.

We started chatting and clicked instantly. Her pearl-white smile contrasted with her smooth tanned complexion, long black hair, and vivid brown eyes, and gave her an angelic look. She reminded me of Princess Jasmine from *Aladdin*.

She told me that her name was Amira and that she had moved to Dubai from a small village in India three years before, after getting married to an IT engineer who worked for a local telecom company. They had been trying for a baby ever since, also undergoing very expensive fertility treatments back home which, however, were not successful.

I could read the pain in her eyes. Her biggest dream was to become a mother. I felt a pang of guilt for having been blessed with a gift that this sweet girl had not been able to experience, and even for needing so desperately some time for myself, when she would have done whatever she could to be in my shoes. But that feeling disappeared quickly when I saw how happy both she and Amal looked, as Amira tickled her and cuddled her in her arms.

We agreed that she would come to our flat every morning to give Amal breakfast, play with her, and take her for a stroll around Discovery Gardens, so that I would have more time to focus on work and attend the conferences I was supposed to take part in for my job. I felt reassured that I had finally found someone reliable and trustworthy who would have been able to look after Amal with love and care, after I had to let go of the eighteen-year-old Italian au pair who had been staying with us for the previous month. Apparently, she had fallen in love with a Syrian boy she had met online a few months before her arrival, and was spending all the time she was expected to take care of the baby chatting on Facebook and arranging their dates.

At first, Tahir and I had tried to be understanding, although we had felt responsible for her safety given that her mother had explicitly asked us to keep an eye on her. We had tried our best to make her feel part of our family, taking her on weekend trips with us, eating out together, and generally making her feel at home. But when, a few weeks into the job, we spotted her flirting with the guy in the opposite section of the overcrowded mall, where we had asked her to meet us once we had got out of the cinema, paying no attention to Amal, who was playing with her feet in the pram a few meters away from her, we felt she had betrayed our trust. We gave her a few days to pack her things, make some arrangements, and leave. That meant I was back to square one, but when Amira and her husband entered our lives, I felt relieved.

We threw a colourful butterfly-themed party to celebrate Amal's first year of life in one of Dubai's largest public parks, together with them and all the other friendly faces who had become a family away from home. A few days after the party, I flew to Rome with Amal to introduce her to her Italian family who were dying to get to know the baby.

I was desperate for a change of air. It had been a very intense year, and I needed a break away from everyday problems, from Tahir's increasingly frequent silences and absent-minded looks, from our financial woes and work pressure, from the overwhelming feeling of living a life which was spiralling out of control.

So, when my sister proposed leaving the baby with my parents for a few days and travelling to the south of Spain together to attend a concert of our favourite Spanish singer, I did not think twice.

"I am in!" I replied excitedly. It had been ages since the two of us had had some girly fun together, both busy with the daily responsibilities of being working mothers and wives.

We had just taken a break in a Moroccan tea house near Cordoba's Mezquita, having spent the whole morning exploring the city's historical district and gossiping about our husbands, when I checked my phone and saw that I had fifteen missed calls from Tahir.

He must have really missed me, I thought, at first surprised that he would be so anxious to talk to me.

But then a more sinister thought crossed my mind. *Is he alright? I hope nothing bad happened to him.*

I called him back straight away, but he did not pick up.

My heartbeat got faster, and I started to get worried. *What if something bad did happen?*

A few minutes later, the phone rang.

"Hello," I answered with an unsteady voice. "Is everything okay?"

"Yes," Tahir replied. "I just wanted to make sure that you are fine and are having a good time."

There was something about his attitude that was totally out of character. He was normally very laid-back and certainly not apprehensive, so I found it quite strange that he would call me fifteen times just to ask me how I was, even more strange at a time in our relationship when he would often look distant and disconnected.

Still, I decided to ignore my gut feeling and believe that, as the saying goes, absence makes the heart grow fonder.

You are overthinking, I told myself. *Give the man a break. He must have simply missed you. After all, he is miles away, all on his own, working hard for the family, while you are on holiday with your sister having the time of your life.*

"We are having a tea near the Mezquita," I told Tahir. "Do you remember?" I said with a lump in my throat.

We had been there together two years before, a few months after we had moved to Dubai, on a ten-day road trip across the whole of Spain to celebrate our second wedding anniversary.

It had been the best holiday ever, not only because Spain was my favourite travel destination, and I was happy I could share my love for that country with him, but also because every single moment had been just perfect, or so it was in my eyes. We had laughed like children, got lost endless times in the Spanish countryside, passionately made love in a traditional guest house opposite Burgos Gothic cathedral, and shared massive T-bone steaks in Santiago de Compostela, as groups of university students dressed in their traditional gowns sang serenades. We had taken in the breathtaking views of Madrid's Art Nouveau buildings at night. Watched a traditional flamenco show inside a cave house in Granada's old gypsy quarter. Engaged in a surreal conversation with the owner of a small family-run restaurant on the way to Segovia, who showed us his vast collection of coins from all over the world and was overjoyed to hear that the Gulf countries had not yet agreed on a common currency. His puzzled face when we had told him that Tahir did not eat pork was priceless. But even more priceless was Tahir's face when, minutes later, he was presented with a large plate of *habas* con *jamón*, fava beans with Serrano ham, which, in the view of our host, did not fall under the pork umbrella. Tahir just smiled and helped himself to some bread and olives instead.

That was what I loved about him. He was just like that: easy-going, uncomplicated, patient. He would very rarely lose his temper.

What had happened to him? Why didn't we seem to be able to have fun together anymore? Why was I starting to feel as if he had already given up on us?

∞

When I returned to Dubai with Amal a couple of weeks later, Tahir was colder than usual. At first, he denied that anything was wrong with him. But after I pressed him for an explanation, he acknowledged that something was indeed bothering him: He had not told me earlier because he did not want to spoil my holiday.

The day he had called me fifteen times while I was in Spain with my sister, he had been in a car accident in Dubai while driving his mum and sisters around to shop for clothes for an upcoming wedding. He had crashed into a Porsche Panamera on Sheikh Zayed Road, Dubai's main artery, but because he had forgotten to renew his car insurance, the police had arrested him and confiscated his passport. His brother had to drive all the way from Muscat to bail him out.

Although it had been a high-speed collision, neither Tahir nor his family members had suffered serious injuries. Tahir had sprained his neck, while his mum and sisters had a few bruises. All of them were still in shock.

The Porsche owner, an Emirati millionaire, had claimed around 180,000 dirhams in damages—approximately Tahir's annual salary— and we had been given a 45,000-dirham quote to repair our own car.

As Tahir was telling me the story, I was overwhelmed with a mix of desperation, dismay, and disbelief. We had been struggling to pay off the loan and move forward with our plans, and just when we had managed to sell the plot of land, the unexpected had happened.

I tried to keep calm, to tell myself that it could have been much worse, that after all, all that mattered was that he was safe and sound, but at that moment, all I could think of was myself. I was tired of making plans for our future that would always go down the drain. I was tired of being patient and understanding, tired of his procrastination. I felt as if we were taking one step forward and ten backwards, and that, no matter how much effort we were making to progress in our lives, we would always end up in the same position. But I felt ashamed for feeling resentful. *We will make it through one more time*, I kept repeating in my head like a mantra, in search for strength to face one more hurdle.

The following morning, we went to see a lawyer to ask for advice on the best way forward. After being charged an exorbitant fee for a twenty-minute consultation, we were told that we had no other option than repaying the Porsche owner in full if we did not want to face legal action and be unable to leave the country.

A few days later, Tahir was asked to appear in court, where he tried to reach an understanding with the claimant. But he was immovable. We eventually gave up, and the next day, we took a cab to the other end of the city, entered a four-storey building in Al Ghurair, which hosted the insurance company the Porsche owner had told Tahir to deliver the money to, and handed in a bag containing the full amount of cash we owed the guy, which we had withdrawn from the bank a few hours earlier. We had only just been able to gather the amount needed thanks to some help from Tahir's siblings and the proceeds from the land sale.

I felt relieved after settling the claim. Debt was not something I had ever experienced first-hand in my life. My parents had a conservative and cautious attitude towards money; they would never spend more than what they had and did not even own a credit card until they were in their sixties. It was thanks to their careful spending that I could enjoy a privileged childhood, attending private schools from an early age, travelling abroad twice a year, and taking part in summer study holidays when I was older.

But Tahir's childhood had been very different. He was born into a large single-income family, where often food was not enough for everybody. His father had died when he was only fourteen which, paradoxically, had allowed him and his siblings to attend college, benefitting from a government grant for children of widows.

His life had been tough but that, in turn, had made him resilient. He would often frown upon my love for fine food, arguing that he could survive on one date a day.

But something had changed inside him since the accident. He was not the same carefree and innocent guy I had met years before. Even his eyes had changed—they had lost their sparkle.

He would spend his days off sitting on the beige fabric sofa that occupied the centre of our living room, resting his feet on the leather coffee table and watching Arabic music channels on the 32-inch plasma TV we had bought on sale from Géant Hypermarket. When he was not watching television, he would work on his laptop or chat to *the clan*, as we jokingly used to call his people, on WhatsApp for hours on end, often late into the night.

Every time I would point out that he was increasingly isolating himself, he would reply that his apathetic behaviour was down to the insomnia triggered by his long and antisocial working hours in the field, combined with the stress from his financial woes and the shock from the car accident. Even when we would go out for a coffee or a meal, he would not engage in a proper conversation. He would just utter a few words, finish his food, and then bury his head in his iPhone again.

One night, as he was working on his laptop, I stood close to him and started stroking his head, resting my lips on his neck to breathe in the musky scent of *Oud*[16] emanating from his skin. I remembered the first time we had been apart, when he had gone back home at the end of his course. I would smell the clothes he had left in my wardrobe several times a day, in a vain attempt to feel him close to me. I would have done anything to go back to that moment. *How could have things changed so much between us?* I could hardly recognise the man I had married.

As soon as Tahir felt the warmth of my skin touching his body, he pushed me away, freezing me with a resentful look.

---

[16] Dark, aromatic resin formed in the heartwood of Aquilaria trees.

"What's wrong with you?" I screamed with exasperation.

"Nothing. You are just disturbing me while I am trying to get some work done," he replied with a disgusted face.

Lately, it would make me feel like everything I was doing was wrong. "I just wanted to give you a cuddle," I muttered, tears of frustration rolling down my cheeks.

I was feeling powerless, hurt from his cold silences and spiteful remarks. I just wanted to bridge the invisible distance separating us and feel he was once again mine. But the harder I would try to get close to him, the stronger he would push me away, driving me insane. We had slowly become two perfect strangers leading parallel lives.

I could not understand where all the resentment he had towards me stemmed from. I felt like *he* was blaming *me* for his mistakes. But what I soon realised was that he was blaming me because he had come to the conclusion that I was his greatest mistake.

If he had not married me, his life would have been different. He would have had the calm and stability he had dreamt of. He would not have to commute long hours to get to work. He would not have wasted his money on a bad investment. If he had lived in Muscat, he could have supervised his project himself rather than having to rely on his brother's help. He could have even avoided the car accident, as he would not have been so tired from driving.

He could have performed *Hajj* in Mecca, with his Muslim wife, who would have taught their children about Islam and would have known how to behave in and outside the house without him having to remind her. They would have fasted together during Ramadan, and she would have cooked the traditional Omani dishes he had been eating all his life, rather than the extravagant recipes his foreign wife would prepare for him. An Omani wife would have accepted to live at home with her in-laws, rather than making him waste money to rent a fancy apartment in Dubai.

Yes, he had it clear: Marrying me had been a huge mistake, the biggest of his life.

He would compare himself to his cousins and siblings who were all living a comfortable life in a stable marriage. Whether they had married for love was not a question that concerned him. Love had only brought him trouble. What he wanted was a woman who would look after him and never question his authority like I used to do most of the time. Someone who would take his word for it and let him focus on his projects without expecting too much in return.

That was what was troubling him most. With me, he was constantly feeling as if he was lagging behind, unable to live up to my expectations. He was feeling under pressure not to let me down, struggling to satisfy my every whim. He would take me to places because *I* loved travelling. He would take me to eat out because *I* loved trying new food. He would take me to the cinema because *I* loved watching films on the big screen. If he could only please himself, he would have been perfectly content to remain in his familiar world made of family gatherings and football matches, 4 x 4 races along Muscat beach, and camping in the desert. He did not need much more than that to be happy. He was living a life which was very different from the one he had imagined and aspired to, and, at that point, he had no doubt that I was responsible for his sense of failure and discontent.

My views, on the other hand, were much more nuanced.

Sometimes, I would also share the same feeling of frustration for not being able to have the kind of close relationship my friends back home had with their husbands, doing basic things like going out for dinner with other couples, having a few drinks on a Friday night, or clubbing until dawn. But above all, I wanted us to be able to make plans for our family without feeling that every decision we would take was somehow dependent on someone else.

CHAPTER NINE

We were reaching a point of no return. He had convinced himself that the only way to save our marriage was moving to Oman and he was trying his best to convince me too.

As far as I was concerned, moving to Dubai had been a mistake, the beginning of the end for our relationship. *We were much happier in England*, I would often tell him.

I missed England, its colours, and smells. The bright yellow of the daffodils in spring, the reddish orange of the autumn leaves falling from the trees onto wet asphalt, the cobalt blue of the sky and the pink sunset of a summer's evening, the lime green of the meadows where cows and sheep would graze. I missed the intense scent of lavender as I walked past the row of semidetached houses on my way to university, the earthy smell of petrichor after a sudden downpour. I missed the wintry skies and the sight of a Gothic church on the gloomy horizon, the greenery sprouting up from a crack in the wall, and the quietness of a Sunday morning stroll.

This is the fate of any immigrant, I thought. A constant sense of longing, of being somewhere and wishing to be somewhere else, because in each place you lived, you left a little piece of yourself that you will never get back. Inside of you are a multitude of identities in relentless conflict with each other, pulling you in different directions, making you doubt who you really are.

Finding a compromise seemed impossible: We were two trains going in opposite directions.

Once, during our first year in Dubai, the oilfield project Tahir was assigned to was completed one day earlier than planned, so he was given that time off. He had driven through the night from Oman just to spend twelve hours with me and then driven back to work the following day. When I opened the door and found him in front of me, I beamed, even more than when I had welcomed him in my arms the day he had taken a chance and moved to London to start a new life together. He had looked so eager to see me, his dreamy eyes filled with love and desire. Now that look seemed to be gone forever, even though my only wish was for him to look at me like that again.

One day at the end of August, while we were arguing over our future plans, as had become the custom over the previous year, Tahir said the words I had never expected to hear. Right up until that moment, he had always made an effort to make up after a fight. No matter how heated the discussion could get, I knew that, at some point, when all was said and done, he would come close to me and put his arms around my shoulders, or give me a little peck on the cheek, to which I would reply with a cross yet forgiving face, reciprocating his gesture in a matter of seconds. That was our secret code. It was like telling each other: *Fair enough. We cannot agree on this and keep driving each other crazy, but we still love each other and will not give up.* But that day, he looked like he had given up.

"I think we should go separate ways," Tahir said in a calm and emotionless tone.

I was gutted. Despite our problems seeming to become bigger day after day, not even once had the idea of splitting up crossed my mind. I had no doubt that the feeling we had for each other was deeper and stronger than any hurdles we were facing, and I was still positive that, sooner or later, we would have found a solution.

I was also unhappy in our marriage, but I thought that growing up meant to stop chasing perfection and accepting that life does not always go as planned. After all, you could not expect people to be as you wanted them to be. No, you could not always have it all. You had to give up something if you wanted to keep something. Rather than fighting for what you aspired to, you needed to fight for what you already had. Happiness was a compromise that you had to make every day because things were rarely, if ever, black and white. *It takes more courage to stay than to leave*, I would tell myself.

But after hearing Tahir talking about divorce, I lost all my courage.

We agreed to take a break. Although I was still working in Dubai, we felt that in our precarious financial situation, it made no sense renting a two-bedroom flat there, when he spent most of his time in the field, and since we could not agree on a common Plan B, we thought that it was better to spend some months apart to think things over with a clear mind.

My employer was looking to fill a correspondent vacancy at the company's Italian bureau, based in Rome. That seemed the perfect chance to get away from Dubai and all the problems of my married life, although it is hard to tell whether I was simply trying to postpone the moment I would need to face up to reality … or perhaps I was just hoping things would eventually sort themselves out.

The plan was to move to Rome with Amal and live with my family for a year, while we saved enough money to repay most of the loan, and perhaps be in a position to look for some other opportunity elsewhere, before our girl, who had just turned two, would be starting school. Tahir would come to visit us every couple of months.

Leaving everything behind to go back to the place I had left when I was just a schoolgirl was as hard as it was to stay.

Having lived on my own for nearly half of my life, I could not help but feel a sense of humiliation and failure moving in with my parents in my thirties, especially since I had always prided myself on being an independent and self-reliant woman.

Unlike me, who passionately defended my right to self-determination, Tahir believed that nobody could be truly independent and that every individual needed the support of his loved ones to succeed in life. That is why family ties were so important to him.

He would often tell me, "If we lived in Muscat, our life would be much easier. My mum could look after Amal when you are busy with work or needed a break. My uncle could help me find a job, my brother could do that, etc. …"

I would get really annoyed every time he said that. I did not want an *easy* life. I wanted a *meaningful* life rooted in the sense of fulfilment that comes from reaching a goal through your own means and efforts. But on that occasion, I was proved wrong. I needed a shoulder to cry on at a time when I was feeling lonely and lost. And to find my direction again, I first needed to know where I had come from.

It was strange sleeping in the same bedroom I had shared with my sister throughout my childhood, in a modest flat on the outskirts of the Eternal City. Everything was still as it was back then: the pink vintage patterned wallpaper covered with school photos and posters of my favourite rock stars; the white wooden shelves displaying teddy bears, textbooks, and postcard collections; the drawers filled with my secret diaries and a few notebooks where I would scribble down dark poems as a teenager; the pink cushions on which I had painted a red floral design for a school project.

Everything was the same, except for me.

I looked around and saw a room and a place that did not belong to me anymore. I could see fragments of a remote past scattered around the house and dusty memories hanging on the walls.

And then, I could see him. His eyes ... that was the problem. They kept talking to me even when I no longer wanted to listen. They seemed to be looking at me even if I did not lift mine. They could open doors I had locked. They could say words his lips could not say. They would keep smiling even when he looked upset. His eyes spoke louder. They answered a question I dared not ask.

CHAPTER TEN

Tahir had come over just before New Year, and as much as we were trying to play happy families in front of Amal, there were too many things left unsaid between us, which could be sensed in the thick and overwhelming tension lingering in the air.

Luckily, my family had decided to spend the last few days of the year at a mountain resort in the Austrian Alps, so that we could make the most of our time alone as a family, totally unaware of the severity of the issues we were facing in our marriage.

On New Year's Eve, as I was playing in the living room with Amal while Tahir was working on his laptop in the kitchen, headphones on, as if he was trying to further isolate himself from the surrounding environment, the phone rang. It was my mum, who had called to wish us a happy new year.

"Your sister is planning for another baby. You should start thinking about that too," she said a couple of minutes into the conversation, with an annoyingly overenthusiastic tone.

"Mum!" I tried to interrupt her before I could say something I would regret, but she continued undisturbed.

"I would love to have more grandchildren before I get too old."

Until that moment, I had not admitted to anybody, not even to myself, that my marriage was going downhill. Admitting that we were on the verge of divorce would make our situation more real, and more painful too. And I was not ready for that.

I was still trying to make sense of our hurdles and find a way to overcome them. I did not want to hear *I had told you* in a fake sympathetic voice. I wanted to give our family another chance. And I wanted to give it to myself too. I could not continue to live at home, waiting for my life to pass without having another go at it.

"Tahir wants a divorce," I told my mum trying to control the stream of emotions that were taking over my body every time the thought of losing him would come to mind.

"*What?!*" my mum shouted in a shocked tone. She had certainly not seen that coming.

In a very short time, Tahir had managed to completely win her over with his charming smile and his kind, courteous, and chivalrous manners, to the point that every time we had an argument, she would always take his side, even before knowing the facts. My father held him in high esteem too.

There was no doubt that he was the son they had always dreamt of having.

"If he had not existed, they should have invented him just for Sofia," my dad used to tease me every time he would catch a glimpse of my beaming smile after a long phone call with Tahir, when, in the first years of our relationship, we would chat into the night like lovebirds do. So, when I told my mum that lately, our discussions would always end with him suggesting splitting up, not only could she not believe her ears, but she blamed me for our problems.

"You are too stubborn. You should be more accommodating and just give in," she argued. She had an old-fashioned idea of how a relationship should work. In her view, marriage was not a loving partnership between two people who work as a team towards a common goal, striving day after day to find a middle ground. On the contrary, she believed that it was the woman's duty to sacrifice herself for her husband and children in order to keep her family united. If that also meant sacrificing her own happiness, it did not really matter. She viewed my worries and doubts as mere tantrums of a spoiled little girl who always wanted to get her way.

On this occasion, however, I had indeed got my way. Tahir had agreed to move back to the UK with me within a year, provided that I could first get a job there, and that I would give him time to sort things back home and also find an opportunity for himself.

I was over the moon. I put all my energy into the job-hunting process, spending several hours a day writing cover letters and polishing my CV. My hard work paid off, and less than three months after we had first agreed on giving our family one last chance and making a fresh start in England, I received a full-time employment offer for a senior reporting role in London.

When I broke the news to Tahir, however, he did not sound too impressed, which in turn spoiled my excitement.

"I told you I will join you and I will, but you cannot expect me to be excited about something I am not too convinced about," he said bluntly.

"It will work out, as long as we stick together," I replied, trying to convince myself as much as him.

∞

As I waited in the Leonardo da Vinci Airport departure lounge to board my British Airways flight to Heathrow, I was swept up in a mix of conflicting feelings. I had left Amal with my parents as I needed some time to look for a flat and day care near my workplace, a five-minute walk from Victoria Station.

I was looking forward to starting afresh, although by moving back to London, where we had shared many happy memories together—as skint as ever, but madly in love—I was actually trying to rewind the tape of my life and chase the shadow of a past that, day after day, was becoming more and more unattainable, and perhaps because of that, increasingly alluring.

Finding decent yet reasonably priced accommodation in a fiercely competitive city such as London proved a bigger challenge than I had expected. In Dubai, I had become used to living in a cosy bubble, a golden cage where everything around me was comfortable at the very least, and luxurious most of the time.

"Look at you! You have become so posh and stylish, just like an Arabian princess," my best friend Lena had told me as soon as she spotted me among the thousands of hurried commuters who, day in day out, inundated Victoria Station's main concourse.

We had not seen each other for four years, since I had quit my city job to board a one-way flight to the Middle East. But despite the distance, we had been updating each other regularly about our lives. I had met Lena ten years before on my university course, and we had clicked from the moment we had exchanged a few words at the end of an English lecture. She was originally from Kosovo and had arrived in the UK when she was twenty-two as an asylum seeker to escape the ethnic cleansing, persecution, and discrimination that had beleaguered her war-torn country.

When she had recounted her story to me, I could not help but think how proud I was to count her among my friends. It was hard to imagine what it had meant for a young student to leave her family, her friends, her studies, her entire life behind to embark on a perilous journey towards the unknown with no guarantees of success. It was impossible to fully comprehend how frightened and hopeless my beautiful friend must have felt as she had crossed the Serbian border, fully aware that a false step would have marked the difference between life and death, heaven and hell, a safe and peaceful existence and one based on fear, intimidation, and abuse.

Her past traumas, though, had not embittered her. She was the kindest and most generous creature I had ever met. During my time in Dubai, she had fallen in love with an Englishman, moved in with him, and had a baby. And in a couple of months, they would finally tie the knot.

"That's great news!" I screamed with excitement as we caught up over a cappuccino in a Belgian coffee chain outside the station. "You deserve all the happiness in this world."

Distance is a state of mind. Some people are physically next to you, but they make you feel like they are a thousand miles away. Others live far from you, but they still manage to get to your heart and warm it up. Lena was one of the latter. No matter how many years would go by or how many miles would separate us, our special bond would never break. Through time and distance, she had been there for me whenever I needed her. She had lived with me through the hurdles I had faced in my marriage, she had celebrated my successes and spurred me on to accomplish even more. Even when she disagreed with my decisions, she would still be ready to offer me a word of encouragement or a pat on the back. When I told her that Tahir and I had taken some time to reflect on the future of our relationship, she was not surprised in the slightest.

I had arrived in London a few days before and spent most of my waking hours looking for a flat that would be big enough for a family of three, would not force me to waste several hours a day commuting to and from work, and would not require robbing a bank in order to pay the rent. My feet were hurting from all the walking, and I was running out of cash. I could not afford to extend my stay at the no-frills yet overpriced B&B near Battersea Park, where I had been staying the first four nights. I needed to find a home and I needed to find it quickly.

As the kind soul she was, Lena invited me to stay at her place until I sorted myself out. At first, I felt uncomfortable accepting, as I was not sure how long it would take me to find what I was looking for and I did not want to upset the balance of her household. But she insisted I could stay as long as I needed, so, as much as I was usually too proud to ask for help, I gave in.

Trying to settle back in London had proved harder than I had imagined. In fact, I had started to believe that it had been a terrible idea, and worse, I had even started doubting that it was what I really wanted. *But what do you want?* I kept asking myself.

I no longer knew. What I did know was that I still loved Tahir. There was not a single shadow of a doubt about that. But was my love enough for both of us? And above all, could we be happy together as we once were? While the magic that once united us had clearly vanished, the straw that broke the camel's back still had to come.

CHAPTER ELEVEN

"I got it! I finally found us a home!" I exclaimed triumphantly.

It had taken me a full week to find the right place, but I was exultant at the thought that soon I could see Amal again and give her and our family a new start.

Tahir still needed more time to finish repaying the loan, but what were six months apart, a year at most, compared to a lifetime together?

"Well done," Tahir replied on the other end of the line. He was about to add something, but he hesitated, as if he was struggling to find the right words.

"What's wrong?" I asked, a feeling of unease pervading my mind.

"I was offered a new job in Muscat. It is an on office-based position. I would be working for a new government agency five days a week. Isn't it great?" he went on, unable to contain the stream of words that had been kept secret for too long and were now flowing freely.

How ironic is that! I thought. Between the two of us, I had always been the one who could talk non-stop about any topic, which had earned me the nickname *Miss Chatterbox* among my friends, but on that occasion, words had failed me.

"You did not want to move to Muscat because you would have spent long periods at home alone while I was in the desert," he said. "But now I have got an office job. I will be back home every evening."

That was not the reason why I did not want to live in Oman. Or at least, it was not the main one. He knew that very well.

"You did not even tell me you were applying for jobs in Muscat," I remarked, voicing all my disappointment. He did not reply, which irritated me further. "So, when were you planning to tell me? I just signed the house contract, found a childminder for Amal, and I am starting my job next week."

"I have not accepted the offer yet," he pointed out in his defence. "What shall I do?"

I was puzzled to say the least. Was he really asking me that question? *He applies for jobs back home behind my back, despite giving me the go-ahead to look for a job in the UK and agreeing to join me within a year, and now, just as I am about to start my new job and settle in, he drops this bombshell on me as if he were asking me to choose what to have for dinner? Why could he not take responsibility for his actions once in a while rather than expect me to decide on his behalf?* But maybe that was exactly what he had been doing by applying for that job, taking back the reins of his life.

"I am not going to tell you what to do," I replied, composed. "It is *your* life. Just do what *you* feel. Not just what feels *right*."

I was about to hang up, but there was one more burning question which, as painful as it was, I had to ask him, even though I knew that the answer could have hurt even more.

"Do you still love me?" I said with a faltering voice. I could hear my heart pounding as I held my breath, waiting for a definitive answer which would hopefully put an end to my prolonged agony. But instead of a dry answer, I was presented with another question.

"What do you think?" Tahir said, sounding slightly annoyed, as if the thought I could doubt his feelings offended him deeply.

"I don't know. It's been a while since you last told me, and I just need to hear that," I replied, overwhelmed by a sense of frustration and hopelessness.

"Of course, I do," he whispered, uneasy to talk about feelings as always. And then he added, his voice filled with sadness: "We just can't be happy together. I think it's better we separate."

Every single word cut through my skin like a sharp blade, travelled through my veins to the stomach, where it burst into raging flames, and finally imploded inside my heart, leaving me drained and empty. Yet, as much as I was struggling to accept the truth, a part of me had already thrown in the towel that very night.

By failing to share his plans with me, I felt he had broken my trust. And what was a relationship without trust? A car without gas, someone said. *You can stay in it as long as you want, but it won't go anywhere.*

In the end, he took the job and travelled to London to visit us for a couple of weeks before starting his new position.

I had rented a one-bedroom flat on the third floor of a Victorian building just opposite Clapham Junction Station and found a childminder who would look after Amal in her home, a few streets away from mine, while I was at work.

The flat was small but cosy, although the lack of lifts made it challenging to carry Amal up and down the stairs in her pram. She was growing fast and had officially entered the *terrible twos* phase with a bang a few months before. I would drop her off at 8 a.m. on my way to work, when she would be too sleepy to walk fast enough, and would often pick her up twelve hours later, finding her so exhausted that she would fall asleep as soon as I put her in the pram.

Like most big cities, London can be tough and unforgiving for many people who arrive there with nothing other than big dreams in their pockets and an unrelenting desire to break through. But for a single working mum who cannot rely on anybody other than herself, it can be even harsher.

It was painful to wave Amal goodbye so early in the morning under a gloomy wintry sky, not being able to see her chirpy smile for the rest of the day, to cuddle each other in bed before having a late breakfast together as we used to do at the weekend, to feel her small puffy hand gently stroking my hair as she whispered *love you* into my ears.

But in those moments, I would suddenly remember the strong women I had met during my time in Dubai, who had no other option than leaving their children in their home countries under the care of a relative, to earn their living working in a variety of roles in the wealthy Gulf states. Many of them were working as maids, cleaners, shop assistants, or beauticians, and were from poorer countries as far away as Sri Lanka, Bangladesh, Philippines, Vietnam, Indonesia, Somalia, and Ethiopia.

I would often ask them about their lives as they gave me a wax at one of the thousands of beauty parlours that had mushroomed across the city. They always seemed keen to share their stories, as if talking about home was the only way to exorcise the bitter nostalgia that was gripping their hearts.

One of them had not seen her two children for almost five years. They were being looked after by their grandma in the Philippines to whom she was sending money every month to cover their expenses. Their dad was an alcoholic who would spend most of her salary on booze and had left them after she had refused to give him any more money to fuel his addiction. She was talking with them regularly over Skype, although it was hard to keep up with their daily lives when they were separated by a few thousand miles, a four-hour time difference, and her busy work schedule. Technology could never replace the closeness of a human touch and even more, the warmth of a maternal hug, but she was comforting herself with the thought that, by working abroad, she would be able to give her children a better future than her own. Two more years of hard work, and she would have saved enough to buy a property in one of Manila's new developments that were flourishing along the seafront.

When she had told me that her youngest daughter was only one when she had left for Dubai and she had to stop breastfeeding her overnight, I was nearly in tears. And now that image was coming back to life as clear as ever inside my head, and I felt silly for finding it so hard to be away from Amal for just a few hours.

Whenever I felt tired of the fast-paced rhythm of my London life, the long office hours, the hustle and bustle of a city that never seemed to sleep, the crowds of strangers who looked so miserable as they threaded their way through the busy railway station concourse, that random thought of those fellow women working away from their children would keep me going. That, and the awareness that, unlike them, I had much more choice. But freedom of choice also comes with responsibilities. And at that point, I did not feel ready to take responsibility for a decision that would not have only affected my life, but also that of the person I loved most.

Having spent most of my childhood with my mother, as my father worked away and was too busy sorting out practical issues when he returned home to find the time to play with his daughter, I did not want Amal to experience the same and grow to see her father as a distant figure who was completely detached from her day-to-day life.

I could not go back in time and I could not go forward. Even after an exhausting day at work, after going back to an empty home, after hurrying to cook a decent meal for Amal and a frozen pizza for myself, after tidying up the flat, which in the morning rush we would leave looking a total mess, dirty clothes spread over an unmade bed and pots and pans left unwashed in the sink. Even then, as I watched Amal collapse next to me in bed after reading her favourite bedtime story, I could not fall asleep, my mind crowded with flashbacks of a past life and a paralysing fear taking hold of my body. I would wonder what Tahir was doing, whether he really missed me as he would sometimes confess, whether he felt as lost as I was. As I tormented myself with these thoughts, I went onto Facebook and started scrolling through my news feed.

Suddenly, I noticed a message from an unknown sender in my inbox. It was from a lady supposedly called Amal, just like my daughter, who had asked me how I was. She said she was from Oman and that she knew my husband. Her profile picture did not show her face but rather a flowery image. There was something fishy about it all. Who was hiding behind that profile? She had no more than ten Facebook friends, but to my surprise, Tahir was one of them. Her account had only been set up a few days earlier. Was it a fake? Was someone using my daughter's name thinking that would have encouraged me to reply? Was Tahir himself trying to test me? No, that was impossible. The Tahir I knew could have never done something like that. I decided to ignore the message and ask Tahir about it the following day, but his reply did not sound very reassuring.

"Just ignore her," he said bluntly in the defensive tone he used every time I asked him a question he did not want to answer. "She is a distant relative in Oman. I will tell her not to bother you," he added, trying to sound as convincing as possible, but as much as I wanted to believe him with all of myself, I just couldn't.

Is he cheating on me?

As hard as I tried, I could not get rid of that sinking feeling.

Instead of calling it quits and admitting to myself that it was better to face up to reality and take a definitive decision, as painful as it could have been, rather than continuing to live in eternal limbo, I chose what, at that moment, sounded like the easiest path.

On one of those sleepless nights, when I was staring at the ceiling in search of an answer I could not find inside of myself, I went back to that message from the mysterious Omani woman. Her account, however, had been deleted, making the seed of doubt that had been planted in my mind grow bigger. On an impulse, I went on Google and typed *relationship*. An array of dating sites started popping up on my screen.

Suddenly, I was pervaded by a mix of shame and guilt. I was about to close all the tabs, but then I tried to convince myself that there was no harm in taking a peek.

After all, my estranged husband was living on another continent and, not only did he not seem to have any intention to join me, but he was also repeating time and again that we should go separate ways. I was angry at Tahir and the condescending attitude he had towards me. And what about that weird message? I was sure there was something behind it I would have not been pleased to hear.

So, I continued browsing through the sites and clicked on one at random. Soon after creating an anonymous and pictureless profile, I started receiving messages from fellow members.

I freaked out. *What the hell was I doing? When exactly had we lost each other? Where had all the promises gone?* I immediately logged off and tried to go back to sleep, once again thinking about Tahir, trying hard to remember how it felt to sleep with him, his arms tightly wrapped around my body in a spooning position throughout the night, as if he were afraid that if he let me go, I would dissolve like salt in water.

"There is only one Sofia in this world. And what would I do without her?" he used to say.

Pity that now he seemed to have found the answer.

CHAPTER TWELVE

The days were going fast between work—the only distraction from all the whys and ifs that tortured my sleepless mind—the household chores, and Amal.

As the hyperactive and restless child she had been even before birth, she was making sure that I never got bored, demanding all the attention I could possibly give her, with the relentless energy and perseverance so typical of toddlers. But the more she would try to push me to the limit by constantly challenging my authority and testing boundaries with temper tantrums that could last for hours on end, the more I would feel guilty for not giving her the emotional stability a child deserves and giving in to her demands more often than I should have done.

I was trying my best to make the most of our free time together. I would take her on weekend trips to Richmond for a stroll along the Thames. I loved watching her staring at the different types of boats that were anchored along the promenade, her eyes wide with amazement. As limited as it was, this quality time together would help make our bond stronger, easing my feeling of guilt.

One day, as I arrived early at work to avoid the rush-hour frenzy, I entered the empty office and sat at my desk, sipping a large cup of strong milky tea, that, together with the pack of digestive biscuits my editor would bring in every day, had become an essential part of my morning ritual.

Suddenly, as I waited for my screen to turn on, I broke down in liberating tears, which prompted my boss, who had walked into the room that very minute, to ask me if I was okay.

I was not, of course, but I had always been very reserved about my private life, so I reassured her that it was just a bad day.

Later in the day, once the tears had given way to an overall feeling of apathy, I received a message from an unknown sender that caught my attention. It was from a guy who had stumbled upon my profile on the dating site and was intrigued by a line I had written about everything happening for a reason. There was something about the way he expressed himself that made him stand out from the crowd. Something I could not really explain, and I was curious to find out.

I felt a sudden urge to reply to his message. Half an hour later, we were chatting away as if we had known each other for a long time. He came across as a genuine and spontaneous person with a positive attitude to life and a dry sense of humour. Still, I was fully aware of the risks of interacting with someone online, that it was so easy to create a fake persona, and that you could not be sure of who was hiding behind a screen until you had met face-to-face.

He invited me for a coffee the following day. I hoped that telling him I was married would put him off. It didn't.

"We can just meet up as friends," he said, with an innocent tone.

Friends? Of course I did not believe even for a second that friendship was what he was after, but I was eager to take my mind off the obsessive thoughts and flashbacks that were flowing inside my head unrestrained, in sharp contrast to the emptiness my heart was trying to fill with a perfect stranger. Talking to someone and letting out my feelings was exactly what I needed at that point, so, after some hesitation, I accepted his invite. We agreed to meet after work outside Clapham Junction Station.

I arrived a few minutes late, feeling nervous and already regretting my decision. I was about to turn back and go home, when I heard someone calling my name.

"Sofia, is that you?" he said, confidently holding a yellow rose in his hand. I smiled timidly. "Are you Jamie?" I enquired. He did not reply but handed me the rose instead.

"Thank you, but you did not have to. We are just meeting as friends, remember?" I pointed out.

We walked up to the nearest coffee shop, where I ordered a green tea, and he had a double espresso.

"I am more of a tea person," I said apologetically, after noticing some disappointment on his face.

"You are Italian and you don't like coffee?" he asked, confused.

"I am atypical on so many levels," I replied, winking at him.

We talked for an hour or so until I told him I had to rush to pick up my daughter from her childminder.

"No worries. I can give you a lift," he said casually as he paid the bill.

"It's okay. It is not so far. I can walk."

"Come on! My car is just a block away. I will drop you off," he insisted.

"Fair enough," I said.

As we walked to the car, checking out the shop windows which were fully adorned in the run-up to Christmas, he took my hand, taking me by surprise. My first instinct was to let go, but I was suddenly imbued with a warm cosy feeling, so I did not move. I felt completely at ease.

Once we reached the car, though, the embarrassment of being in an intimate situation with a complete stranger prevailed, and I closed my eyes pretending to feel very tired.

When I opened them again, I found him staring at me, our lips a whisper apart.

"What are you doing?" I asked.

"I was trying to kiss you. I have been thinking about that since the first moment I saw you."

I pushed him away, urging him not to get close, although my eyes betrayed me, revealing my restrained desire.

He apologised and kept quiet for the rest of the journey. Then, once we arrived, he got out of the car and opened the door for me.

"Thanks for the lovely afternoon. It was great seeing you. Let's do it again," he said as he leaned forward to give me a hug and a peck on the cheek. He smelled of cigarettes and cologne.

I gave him a perplexed look. "Let's see," I said, not wanting to make any promises which I was not supposed to keep.

As I crossed the street and stopped in front of the childminder's house, I looked back. He was still there. He waved at me and threw kisses in the air. I waved back, embarrassed, then he got back into the car and drove away.

Later that night, as I was making dinner for Amal who was sitting quietly in her little lime green armchair, watching her favourite CBeebies show with a concentrated face, Jamie rang me.

"I really like you," he said with a confident and slightly presumptuous tone.

"Look, I really enjoyed talking to you today. But my life is a complete mess at the moment, and I don't want to complicate it further."

"I understand. But you don't have to," he replied leaving me even more confused. "Let's get to know each other and just see what happens. I think that would help you stop overthinking."

Maybe he is right, I thought. *I just think too much. I should take it easy and go with the flow*, and from that moment, I tried to enjoy our time together. However, those fun and carefree rendezvous were tainted by an oppressive feeling of guilt and shame for trying to run away from my past by holding onto a fleeting moment, rather than face the truth and take a decision which was slowly crystallising in my heart.

∞

Jamie was fun and charming, and had deep almond-shaped black eyes and a dimple on his face that gave him a cheeky look. He was one of those people who have a carefree but not careless attitude to life. Who don't overcomplicate things and make you feel one hundred per cent yourself. Who say the first thing that comes to their mind. Who, if they have a problem with you, tell you straight away rather than talk behind your back. Who do not plan every single minute of their lives and do not stress over petty things. Those who, when they say something nice, really mean it. Those who hate formalities. Who, if you invite them for dinner, do not really care if you are going to have a takeaway pizza or eat in a Michelin-starred restaurant, as long as you have a good time together. Who can live in the present and savour every moment rather than spend every minute worrying about the next. Someone with whom you do not have to weigh your words for fear of being misunderstood. Who can live and let live.

When I looked at him as he laughed over a joke he had just finished telling me, I would think that, if the world had more of this kind of people, life would be much easier.

We would meet each other often for a coffee after work, until one day he invited me for dinner at his place.

"I will make the best roast dinner you have ever tasted," he announced confidently. "And I am not going to accept no for an answer," he added, winking at me.

The idea of a guy treating me to a homemade dinner prepared by his lovely hands was very appealing, especially at a time when, most nights, I arrived home so exhausted that I would eat anything that could be ready in no more than ten minutes, and, most of the time, would come straight from a packet.

But I was not fooling myself either. I knew very well that going to his place could also mean crossing the limits between a mere yet tempting possibility and an irreversible and unforgettable certainty, which, as alluring and exciting as it was, would have opened a Pandora's box of regret, guilt, and shame.

And so it was.

Later that night, as I gathered my clothes scattered across the floor, I gave Jamie one last goodbye hug without saying a word, already trying to erase the memory of him and our secret moment of wildness from my heart and my mind. Then I closed the door behind me, trying to compose myself, and hailed a taxi outside his apartment.

I was eager to go back home to Amal, who was being looked after by my friend Lena, and bury myself under the warm woollen blankets, hoping that the frosty December night would freeze my brain and delete any trace of my betrayal by the morning, hiding it under a thick layer of snow.

The next day, after a sleepless night, I handed in my resignation. I decided to go back to Rome for some time to reflect on what had happened and where to go from there. I needed to stop talking in order to hear what my inner voice had to say.

It was reassuring to be able to go back to a familiar place which could be called home, a safe haven where you could return to every time you would feel lost, although I was no longer sure whether such a place did really exist outside of my imagination.

When was the last time I had felt home in my endless wandering?

I had got out of my comfort zone and tested my limits so many times that I no longer knew where I belonged.

I closed my eyes and was transported to a different time when, no older than four, I was eating pomegranate seeds for the very first time in the kitchen of Mrs Luisa, the neighbour who was looking after me when my mum was at work until I started school.

Mrs Luisa was a gentle soul who lived in our building together with her husband, who worked from home as a tailor, their two boys, and her in-laws. I used to love spending the mornings helping her prepare lunch for the family, watching her with a mix of wonder and deep admiration as she chopped the vegetables, which I had rinsed for her, on the large wooden chopping board on full display near the window.

I was impressed by how everything she would make always tasted so delicious, especially the tomato *passata* she would prepare from scratch, slow-cooking tomatoes together with carrots, celery, and a few secret ingredients.

As a fussy eater, I would always wonder why everything prepared by Mrs Luisa tasted and looked much better than my mum's food, which she would scrape together after picking up my sister from school on her way back from work.

I remember that, one day, as soon as I arrived home, my mum and sister told me that Mrs Luisa had brought me a bowl of pasta soup she had made that morning for lunch, as she would often do.

My eyes beamed with excitement. I went straight into the bathroom to wash my hands and emptied my plate at light speed, praising the cook for her great culinary skills. As soon as I finished, they told me that the soup had actually been made by my mum and that they wanted to see my reaction, as I always complained about her cooking.

That very day I learned that what makes something taste as good as home is not just the ingredients, but the amount of love one puts in it.

In Mrs Luisa's house, where I learned to sew from her husband, having fun at patching leftover fabric scraps together, where their two sons threw me in the air and made me fly, where the whole family talked, joked, and laughed when they gathered around the dinner table, religiously sticking to a no-TV rule at mealtimes, I felt at home, comfortably cocooned in the safety of their happy and loving household.

On those occasions, I also realised that family is not necessarily defined by blood ties. Family is someone who makes you feel at home.

But what home means is entirely subjective. I spent most of my youth looking for that feeling of protection and safety I had experienced in Mrs Luisa's family, which was such a stark contrast from the frenzy of my own, only to realise that the feeling I was so desperately craving was already inside me. But only the right person would be able to bring it to the surface.

CHAPTER THIRTEEN

Lena listened to me carefully as I told her what had happened between Jamie and me. Then, after making sure I had nothing more to add, she took a deep breath and gave me an understanding look, one of those looks filled with empathy and forgiveness that true friends give you when you need them most. That was what I loved most about her. She was one of the few people I had met in my life who never made me feel judged. She knew all too well that I was tormented enough by my own regrets, so she did her best to avoid rubbing salt into my wounds.

"It's okay, *girlie*," she said as she stroked my back. "I think you just need to take some time off to focus on yourself and decide what it is that you really want. You cannot go on like this any longer. Sooner or later it will get at you," she added, with the sensible pragmatism of a woman who had seen it all in life, to the point that little—if anything—could surprise her.

"You're right, Lena. The trouble is … I feel so lost. I always thought I knew what I wanted, but now I no longer know the answer. All I wish is to go back in time and be happy again."

"For a start, you should stop idealising the past. Are you sure you were really happy *before*?" she enquired, giving a voice to the doubts that had already started to gain ground in my subconscious.

I could not answer her question. Not before digging inside myself.

"Good luck, Sofia. I wish you will soon find what you are looking for," Lena said as she saw me off at Heathrow Airport, while I was about to embark on a trip back home that felt like a personal failure.

"I hope I'll find it too," I replied with a hint of scepticism.

Her dark brown eyes followed me as I walked through the security checks, firmly holding Amal's hand on one side and, on the other, a trolley bag packed with nappies, a set of spare clothes, wet wipes, travel-size toiletries, a couple of books, and all the other essentials a woman's handbag is not big enough to contain.

The first few days back home were hard, as I tried to make sense of the previous seven months and decide where to go from there.

My boss had been very understanding. She knew that something was troubling me deeply and even offered for me to continue to work for them remotely for some time until I had figured out what to do.

It did not take too long, though, for that to happen. I followed very few rules in my life, but one of them was that I preferred regretting something I had done rather than something I had not. The other rule was to be always true to myself, although I was firmly convinced that truth was a relative concept which varied according to the perspective from which one looked at reality. I did not want to move forward with my life before being able to tell myself that I had done all I could have possibly done to save my marriage.

I had made up my mind. I would tell Tahir everything I felt, including that I had met someone in London and we had started a relationship and, hopefully, he would understand me or even forgive me, and we would try to start again from there.

I wanted us to be fully honest with each other and tell each other anything that may have happened during our time apart. I wanted us to be able to look into each other's eyes again without any shame or distrust. It would not be easy and it might not work. After all, it was impossible to go back in time, but at least we would have nothing to recriminate, so, when Tahir came over to visit us during the Eid holidays, I told him all my heart could say. I told him that I wanted to give our family one more chance and that I had decided to leave everything behind and move to Muscat by the summer to try and build a new life together. I was doing it for us but also for myself. I was a fighter and I needed to prove to myself that I would fight my battle until the very last bullet.

I told him how lost and lonely I had felt in London, that I had met a friendly face that had initially managed to ease my feeling of emptiness, giving me the care and attention I once received from my husband, and that I had grabbed them with all of my strength; however, when things had progressed beyond friendship, I had felt emptier than ever before, overwhelmed by lacerating guilt for having tainted the pureness of our love.

Tahir listened to my story quietly, his poker face not giving away any emotions, not even when I started crying like a baby. He did not talk. Instead, he started stroking my arms gently as I sat on his lap, wiping my tears with his hands. I guess it was his way to tell me that he still considered me his.

I knew he was too proud to ever accept the idea that his wife had cheated on him. Particularly considering that he came from a polygamous culture where it was acceptable, and still relatively common, for a man to have more than one wife. However, extramarital relationships, and even worse if the adulterous party was a woman, were seen as one of the most immoral crimes a person could ever commit, even though that did not prevent them from happening, albeit in a much more discreet way than in the West.

If he had told his family what I had done, they would have certainly pushed him to divorce me. In fact, they could not even figure out why I was away from my husband in the first place. Why I had not accepted to settle down where the head of my household wanted to. To them, it was very clear: A wife follows her husband and obeys him. That was how it was supposed to be. There was nothing to discuss.

But after all, if my own *Western* family thought the same, how could I expect that Tahir's family, who belonged to a much more traditional society, would think differently? No, I couldn't. I had to understand and accept that they would never relate to my way of thinking.

One day, Tahir told me that one of his older sisters, who was married with kids, had been offered a scholarship by her employer to pursue a one-year master's degree at a top-notch Australian university.

I was so excited for her. I immediately told Tahir that he should encourage her to accept the scholarship because it was a once-in-a-lifetime chance. That her children, some of whom were already teenagers, could have stayed with her husband. That one year goes very fast, and if they missed each other, they could have still met during the holidays.

In the end, she turned down the offer. I would have accepted her decision if it had truly been her own, but when I heard that her husband *had not let her go*, as Tahir had put it, and worse, that less than a year later, he had himself left his wife and children behind to study on a two-year course in the UK, my heart revolted like it did every time I felt some injustice had been committed.

I voiced my disappointment to Tahir, who partly agreed with me, but he did not share my rebellious spirit. He did not dare challenge the unwritten social norms under which he had been brought up. He was used to conforming to a society where everybody wore the same clothes, practised the same religion, and spoke the same language, and if someone stood out from the crowd, it was, more often than not, for the wrong reasons. Being different made him feel uncomfortable, just like in public situations, having a foreign wife embarrassed him; it made it harder to keep a low profile, one in line with his reserved nature. And as much as I often felt humiliated by his attitude, like the times he wanted to hide my hair behind a veil in order not to attract unwanted attention, I did understand him.

But on this occasion, it was just me and him inside the hotel room we had been sleeping in, on a weekend away to the Tuscan hills I had organised to celebrate his birthday, even though I knew that, before meeting me, he was not accustomed to celebrating such a festivity. But I enjoyed spoiling my loved ones and even myself on such occasions, and I felt that being alone for a couple of days in a relaxing environment would give us an opportunity to talk things through and maybe even reconnect.

My parents had promptly accepted to look after Amal and, although it was always difficult to be away from her, I was also glad that we could have an honest overdue conversation without worrying that she might hear what we had to say. But it was not exactly going as I had expected. In fact, I felt that more than a conversation, it was a monologue.

"I don't want to lose you," I sobbed, although in all truth, I knew I had already lost him.

I had opened up to Tahir, feeling more vulnerable than ever, in the hope that he would do the same, and that we could slowly rebuild the trust that no longer existed between us.

I would have preferred that he got mad at me, screamed at the top of his lungs, told me to get lost. Whereas, he was silent, and his silence was making me feel even more guilty and more uncomfortable, because the moment anger turns into indifference, you know it's over.

Did he really love me so much that he could not hate me even after what I had told him? Or was he silent because it would have been hypocritical to make me feel bad for something he had also done?

These doubts were killing me, but there was no point in asking him. I knew that he would have never answered me anyway. Even when I had asked him about that weird message on Facebook, he denied he had done anything wrong. All I could do, if I really wanted us to start afresh, was sweep my doubts under the carpet and believe him.

And that is what I tried to do.

A few days before Tahir's arrival, I had gone out late in the afternoon to avoid the intense heat of the Roman summer, which was making me feel edgier and more restless than I already was. I had headed straight to the big jewellery shop located on a busy dual carriageway connecting the eastern part of the city to the main university area.

Half an hour later, I came out of the shop carrying a gift box containing my birthday gift to Tahir. It was a silver wedding ring—to replace the one Tahir had lost when he was in the field. A date was engraved on the inside of the ring: 20 June 2015, the day on which I would have given him the ring on the occasion of his birthday.

I had chosen that date for a few reasons. I wanted our marriage to be born once again, like a phoenix is born again from the ashes of its predecessor. And was there a better day to mark the renewal of our commitment to each other than his birthday?

On his special day, I wanted to give him the most precious gift I could possibly think of: A new me, ready to offer him my love, trust, and support once again, to leave the past behind and embark on a new journey together.

However, when I finally gave him the ring, and he tried it on, I realised it was too loose. Embarrassed, I promised him I would take it back to the jewellery shop and have it tightened as soon as we got back to Rome; but as I struggled to fall asleep later that night, I wondered whether that was a sign of things to come, whether our marriage was just like a poorly tailored suit that, no matter how many alterations one makes, will never fit properly.

CHAPTER FOURTEEN

As I had promised, Amal and I joined Tahir in Muscat at the end of the summer.

Years before, I had boarded the same Emirates flight to embark on a new adventure in the Middle East. Same route but different life, hopes, and expectations. But now I was travelling back to that part of me, the part that had never really left. I knew that there would have been plenty of bumps along the road ahead, but I was also fully aware that if I had not driven that road, I would have never found out. And I could not wait to be in the driving seat.

When I spotted Tahir in the arrival hall of Muscat International Airport, looking smart in his light blue dishdasha and matching hand-embroidered *kuma*[17], I thought that we were once again a family, and that very thought was enough to fill my heart with the same pride I experienced on the day we married.

As soon as he saw us, he walked in our direction as Amal ran towards him, her cute little face beaming with excitement. Tahir picked her up and the two of them shared one of those intense father-daughter moments that remain in a child's memory for the rest of their life.

When I reached them, he gave me a timid hug to which I responded with a much tighter one, which lasted longer than it was supposed to, as I realised from the curious stares we received from the noisy crowd of people gathered around the arrival gate.

---

[17] Traditional cap worn by Omani men.

How many times had Tahir told me to avoid displays of affection in public places? So many times that I had lost count, but even if he repeated that one more time, it would have made little difference. Expecting someone as emotional as me to control their feelings because they could hurt someone's sensibilities was too much to ask. The way I saw it, being able to express oneself was what differentiated humans from robots. I failed to understand how the sight of two people showing affection for each other could hurt, annoy, or offend a passer-by.

Tahir let go of my arms to help me with the bags.

We had rented a modern one-bedroom flat in a mixed-use development along Muscat waterfront, where most of the city's expat community lived, comprising a small shopping centre, restaurants, hotels, private access to the beach, and even a bilingual nursery for Amal. It was the perfect family-friendly place to start our new life together, although I soon realised that what makes a place beautiful are the people who surround you. And lately, when I was in Tahir's company, I was often feeling lonelier than when I was alone.

At first, I silenced that inner voice, trying my best to arrange activities that we could enjoy as a family, like lazy afternoons on the beach, off-road trips to the *wadis*,[18] strolls in Qurum Natural Park, and culinary experiments in our new kitchen. But regardless of what we were doing, the voice was growing louder.

I felt Tahir was taking part in our activities out of a sense of duty, but his mind always seemed to be somewhere else. He seemed much more preoccupied with his physical appearance, covering the first white hair that peeked out from his beard and sweating at the gym to get a perfectly shaped six-pack, than with our marriage, in what to me seemed an early-onset midlife crisis.

"To me, you still look perfect even with some white hair and a fuller belly," I would often tell him to try and reassure him. But maybe it was not my attention that he was trying to attract with his meticulous grooming.

---

[18] The bed or valley of a stream in regions of southwestern Asia and northern Africa that is usually dry except during the rainy season and that often forms an oasis.

From the very first week, he juggled himself between work, football matches with his mates, Friday gatherings at his mum's place, social commitments such as weddings and engagements, his workouts, daily visits to the local mosque, and of course, us.

Having been apart for such a long time, he had started enjoying the perks of the bachelor life, where there was no one he had to be accountable to other than himself. He suddenly felt overwhelmed by the burden of his new responsibilities and started going out even more often to reclaim his lost freedom.

I, on the other hand, felt he had not given my decision to move to Muscat the right importance and was taking me for granted. He knew all too well how hard it had been for me to take that step, and if I had done it, it was because a part of me still believed in us.

The other part was telling me that it was already too late and that his bored, lifeless expression when we were spending time together was proof of that.

"If you keep ignoring me, I'd better leave," I would tell him out of desperation, but he did not seem to take my threats seriously. Or maybe, that was exactly the reaction he was hoping to provoke with his passive attitude, although he could not bring himself to admit it just yet.

One day, Tahir left home early to drop off Amal at the nursery before going to work. I gave both a kiss, wishing them a good day and then cleared the table, before sinking into the magnolia IKEA sofa bed opposite our balcony, from which I could enjoy spectacular views of the Arabian Sea. Suddenly, as I bit into the egg sandwich I had made for breakfast, I noticed that Tahir had left his phone on the coffee table.

Worried that he would be unable to communicate, I took the phone thinking of a way I could get it delivered to his office. But then I realised it was his spare phone, not the one he used on a day-to-day basis. Breathing a sigh of relief, I was about to put the phone down when I saw that, unlike his other phone, it did not require an access password. A sudden thought crossed my mind.

Don't even think that! Checking your husband's phone? That is really mean, and it is not what a healthy relationship should be based on, I tried to convince myself.

But my frustration with Tahir's silences and the need to know once and for all what was really going on inside his head was too tempting, so I started browsing through it.

Ten minutes later, feeling silly and ashamed for having doubted him, when I had found nothing on his phone that could have put our marriage at risk, I began closing all of the tabs I had opened, one by one, promising myself never to do something like that again. But just as I was closing the last tab, a new window popped up to notify Tahir of a new message from a girl called Layla. With shaky hands and a racing heart, I clicked on the message, only to discover that it was just the latest in a series of hundreds of text exchanges between him and other female members of a dating social network.

I was gutted. Around half of the messages were in Arabic, which made it impossible for me to read them, but the other half were in English, as many of the girls Tahir had interacted with lived outside of Oman.

As I skimmed through the messages, I felt a mix of humiliation, disgust, and heart-wrenching pain. *What did these girls have that I could not give him?* was my first thought. *What had happened to the man I married?* Maybe the same that happened to the woman he married, an inner voice promptly replied. We had lost each other, and those messages were just the tip of an iceberg that had been melting day after day, leaving us stranded at sea, desperately looking for a safe harbour where we could give our tired souls a break from their endless wandering.

For the following few hours, I cried until there was not a single tear left. The reason for my tears was not the feeling of betrayal, not even the fact that, before our arrival in Muscat, my husband had invited an unknown woman for a drink at our place, the place that was supposed to be the setting of our new life together. Not even that when she had declined the invite, he had insisted further. Not even that his dating profile showed pictures of him that I had personally taken on our latest family holiday. Not even that he had taken some years off his real age and modified his personal data in order to attract more attention.

None of that really mattered to me. Judging him would have been hypocritical considering that I had given him tit for tat.

What really tore me apart was the awareness that there was no way back, that what we once had, everything we had tried to build in nearly a decade of our lives, no longer existed. And nothing we could say or do would have brought it back.

It was the final chapter of a beautiful story of love and passion, of days we could not take our eyes off each other and days we just wanted to be left alone. Of moments when we would laugh together, and others when we would laugh at each other. Of bitter fights followed by tender reconciliations, of cosy dinner dates and movie nights, hand-in-hand strolls on the beach and chilled-out weekends, of late breakfasts smelling of milky cardamom tea and paratha bread, of nostalgic Arabic tunes played out loud on Tahir's phone while he took hour-long baths and Latin songs played on mine as I did the same.

Of afternoons when the desire we had for each other was so strong that no work or study commitment could ever restrain it. Of nights when his arms were all I needed to let go of any fear.

From now on, our lives would no longer be intertwined. We would walk along different paths, at different paces, slowly turning into the perfect strangers we had allowed to access our private space and destroy the sacredness of our union.

When Tahir got back from work, a couple of hours before we were due to pick up Amal from her swimming lesson, he found a scene he had certainly not expected.

I was sitting on the sofa, from where I had not been able to move for the previous few hours, my puffy eyes fixed on the floor to avoid giving away the whirlwind of emotions he would have read into them.

I was not sure I had the strength to confront him at that point, so I kept quiet and let the facts talk by themselves.

"What happened?" Tahir asked me in shock as soon as he opened the door and realised how miserable I was.

I thought telling him that I had found his phone would have been enough to get the message across and would have immediately prompted him to ask for forgiveness with a repentant tone. But to my surprise, the first thing he did was tell me off for having damaged the screen after pressing the buttons too hard, hoping that, by doing so, the words already stuck in my mind would vanish like a bad dream.

"I am telling you I discovered your chats with other girls and all you worry about is a bloody phone?" I shouted, incandescent with rage. I was shocked to say the least, but inside me there lingered a tiny bit of hope that he would come to his senses and apologise. However, I had not taken into account how deep-rooted his belief was that a man should never show vulnerability in front a woman. It was a sign of weakness that would have made him lose face and respect.

He reacted in the only possible way his pride allowed him to. Instead of admitting that he had done something wrong, he just played down the seriousness of the situation.

"It was nothing. It was just a bit of fun, nothing happened. But you should not have spied on my phone," he said with a patronising tone.

"So, inviting a girl for a drink inside your home when your wife is away is *nothing* to you? If nothing happened, it's just because she did not accept your invitation. And I already know I should not have read your messages. Still, I am really glad I did," I yelled among the tears.

"You did worse than that," he replied matter-of-factly.

Here we were. I thought that moving to Oman for him was the greatest proof of love I could have possibly given him. That he had finally understood how important he was to me, that I had realised my mistakes and was ready to leave them behind and move on together. But in reality, he had not missed a chance to throw them back in my face. I had tried to be honest with him and tell him what had happened with Jamie because I did not want to start a new chapter on the wrong foot. How could I be sure he had not hidden something and was now bringing up the past to divert my attention from his own mistakes and make me feel even guiltier than I already felt?

They say real love knows no pride. And maybe that is true. If two people are not willing to give and take, to reach a middle ground day in, day out, to forgive each other for their mistakes and learn from them, to set their egos aside for their mutual good, they are unlikely to build a trusting, solid, and loving relationship.

From that day onward, we started leading separate lives. He would go out with his friends and family after work, while I would meet up every afternoon with other expats who lived in our community.

Amal was equally happy to spend time with her paternal family at her grandmother's house, as she was to take part in the playdates I would arrange with the other children from the nursery, or to join me as I went for a coffee with my girlfriends, unaware that her parents would soon stop sharing the bed where she peacefully slept every night, feeling cosy and safe as our arms wrapped her small body in a warm embrace.

It was nearly Christmas, and as I prepared myself to spend the holidays with my family, I knew that once I had boarded that flight, I would not look back. Tahir knew it too, but he did not do anything to stop me. And in hindsight, I am grateful to him for that.

Back home, as I asked myself time and again what was holding me back from taking a step that had been written on my heart for a long time, I read a line from a psychology book Lena had given me just before leaving London. The book was saying that every time we are at a crossroads in our lives, unsure about our future goals, we should take the path that scares us most, because our greatest fears also hide our greatest desires[19]. After reading that sentence, I felt that I had finally found the answer I had been looking for, and the heavy cloud I was engulfed in, lifted and vanished over the horizon.

---

[19] The book *"Las gafas de la felicidad"* by Spanish psychologist Rafael Santandreu (1969–).

CHAPTER FIFTEEN

I moved back to the UK just after New Year's. After all, that's the time of the year when people tend to take stock of their lives and make new resolutions. Just like them, as I was slowly coming to terms with my decision, I had drawn a list of goals I wanted to achieve in the following twelve months.

One of them was buying my own place in Leeds, a city where I had spent five of the most beautiful years of my life as a student and I had found myself for the first time ever.

As I had walked down its streets fifteen years before, despite feeling a stranger among strangers, I had experienced a sense of belonging and connection to the place, which was still considered slightly remote and isolated back then.

This is my place, I remember thinking as I arrived at Kirkstall Brewery, the university's hall of residence where I had lived during the first few months of my student life. I had been both excited and terrified at the idea of being completely on my own in a foreign country, where people spoke a language I had learned in school textbooks with an accent which was totally different from the posh Queen's English my teacher used to speak.

But as the days went by, my confidence had slowly started to grow, to the point that I had decided to take up a weekend job as a shop assistant in a local bakery chain to ease the feeling of loneliness and homesickness I often experienced when I had no lectures to attend.

It was my very first interaction with the adult world, a world of responsibilities and deadlines, where there was nobody other than yourself to rely on, no mum to prepare your meals or wash your clothes, no elder siblings to ask for an opinion when you could not make up your mind, no childhood friends to cheer you up when you were feeling low.

But on the other hand, there were many more things to look forward to. There was the freedom of doing whatever pleased you without anybody feeling entitled to give you unsolicited advice. There was the sense of empowerment stemming from awareness that, by choosing to study miles away from home, you had taken control of your young life and decided what kind of individual you wanted to become. Did you want to be a fearful and insecure person who would never have the guts to step out of her comfort zone and just take a chance? Or did you want to be someone who faced her fears even if that scared the hell out of her?

Even then, as I approached the adult world with a mix of apprehension and hesitation, I knew who I wanted to become. And something inside me told me that Leeds, with its beautiful parks and plainspoken residents, strangers acknowledging your existence by calling you *luv*, lively student population and vibrant nightlife, was the right place to be anything I wanted.

It was a city pulsating with life, which on the one hand, was attached to its traditions and was striving to preserve them, and on the other hand, was slowly looking to the future. It was very different from the Leeds of the forties, which Alan Bennett had superbly described in one of his most famous quotes as a place where "life is generally something that happens elsewhere."[20]

The Leeds I knew was a place where the authenticity and quiet of country life blended perfectly with the hustle and bustle of city life, where locals could at first be a little suspicious towards outsiders but, in no time, they would let down their barriers to reveal a friendly and welcoming nature. So, when years later, I found myself staring at a world map to choose the setting for the next chapter of my life, I had no doubts that Leeds was the place where I wanted to build my future.

---

[20] From *Telling Tales* (2000) by Leeds-born author Alan Bennett (1934–).

These were my thoughts as I walked into town, past Hyde Park and the ancient university buildings. I have always enjoyed walking. It helps me relax and look at things under a different light. Every time I had been nervous about something or had an important decision to make, I would go for a brisk walk and find refuge among the sturdy trees scattered around the park, watching sweaty joggers as they stretched after an early morning run, children chasing each other in the playground, couples holding hands as the world went by. I would be washed in a profound sense of calm knowing that, no matter how things would go, or how my life would change, that park would still be there as a reassuring presence amidst the precarity of life.

How many secrets must have been shielded by those trees? How many stories must have been written on their trunks? How many storms must they have weathered? I would wonder. But here they were, stronger and more resilient than ever, just like us, wonderful human beings, so fragile in our transient existence, and yet eternal fighters who never give up, even in the most desperate of times, even when we feel defenceless before an evil more cunning than us. Even then, when everything seems lost, we keep fighting with dignity, and it is precisely *then*, when we feel overwhelmed with a sense of despair, that our most authentic nature comes to life.

What extraordinary creatures human beings are. If only we could realise that early in our lives, rather than wasting years yearning for a past which will never come back. Or missing out on precious opportunities as the paralysing fear of failing and making a fool of ourselves takes control of our restless minds.

There I was, back in a city I loved, ready to embark on a new, unknown life journey and start from scratch, as I had done the first time I arrived in this country. I was feeling just like those trees. Still ready to fight on, even with a broken heart and a bruised soul, even if the fear of falling again would keep me awake at night and crowd my dreams with fragmented memories from a past life that no longer belonged to me, leaving me in a state of anguish and exhaustion that would linger for the rest of the day.

Despite the way things had ended between us, Tahir and I had separated on amicable terms. He was happy for me to settle down in England with Amal, promising her that he would visit her regularly, a promise he kept for the following years.

It was hard to see him arrive at our place, tired and weary after an eight-hour flight, and not be able to hold him in my arms as I used to do when he would come back from his shifts in the desert, aware that, soon, other arms would have comforted him instead of mine. To smell the exotic scent of sandalwood and frankincense that emanated from his clothes, permeating the entire house and lingering in the air for days after he had left, as an ethereal presence which could not be touched but could still be felt. To resist the attraction that was still alive and kicking between us, to the point that, on some occasions, our impulses prevailed, eroding all of the certainty on which I was building the foundations of my new life, one brick at a time.

"You should set some boundaries," Lena said, when I confessed that Tahir and I still desired each other. "You are just going to hurt yourself."

She was right. I needed some closure, although I was not sure that a piece of paper would have been enough to sever the bond that was still uniting us.

On a rainy November afternoon, I plucked up the courage, got into a cab, and headed into town, stopping in front of a building near the courthouse. What I remember of that gloomy day was the smell of petrichor emanating from the wet asphalt, one of my favourite smells since I was a child. I had loved watching the rain hitting the ground from my sixth-floor bedroom. It overlooked a large courtyard where flocks of pigeons would gather to gobble up the tiny breadcrumbs my neighbours would shake off tablecloths from their balconies after meals. Rain to me meant movement, and movement meant life. The loud yet constant sound of a downpour felt reassuring, muffling any other noise, including my own thoughts. How ironic it was that, on one of the saddest days of my life, the power of nature was still able to evoke such sweet images, as a subtle reminder that, even when everything goes wrong, there is always a reason to smile.

The divorce lawyer I had spoken to on the phone the previous morning was waiting for me in an impersonal meeting room on the first floor of the building, looking professional and impeccable in her tailored navy-blue suit and matching leather pumps.

I, on the other hand, with my puffy eyes, untamed hair, and shabby clothes, felt like a hot mess.

Shortly after I sat down, she asked me to relate the story of my marriage to her, in order to find some faults in Tahir's behaviour that could form the basis of my divorce petition.

As if the pain of separating from the man I had loved most in my life, seeing the family we had built with such a great effort, going against everything and everybody to be together, fall to pieces, was not a burden heavy enough to carry. Now, I was asked to relive my pain with a complete stranger, who was not eager to listen out of compassion, but rather to identify flaws in Tahir's character that would allow her to hold him legally responsible for the end of our marriage. *This is too much to bear*, I thought, as the tears started flowing without me even realising it.

I was about to get up and leave, when I remembered the promise I had made to myself as I prepared to move out of my parents' house for the very first time: *Don't ever run away from your fears. Otherwise, they will only get bigger and bigger.*

I took a deep breath, told her my story, and told myself that this horrible moment would soon be over, pleading with her to make the process as fast and painless as it could be. I did not want anybody to taint the memory of what we had once been. I wanted to cherish those unforgettable moments for myself and nobody else.

There are no winners or losers in a break-up. There are just two people who tried their best to make it work, but they couldn't. And that is not necessarily someone's fault. It is just that, often, people love in different ways, but they *expect* to be loved in the way they *want* to be loved. And as someone said, expectation is the root of all evil. What happened next was living proof of that.

Miad

CHAPTER SIXTEEN

"I know you have had a bad experience, but do not think that all men are the same," you told me after I finished telling you my story. You had noticed how the tone of my voice would change every time I talked about the past. In fact, I could not mention my ex-husband without feeling a lump in my throat.

That men were all the same, or better said, that they were all like Tahir, was precisely what I hoped, given that, since my divorce, I would look for him in the eyes of every man I met. I could not stop comparing them to him because, despite everything, Tahir was still the only man I wanted.

I would go on a date thinking how Tahir would have behaved in the same situation. Would he have opened the door for me? Would he have given me his jacket if I told him I was cold? Would he have texted me as soon as he got back home to make sure I was okay? *What would he have said? What would he have done?* And any man whose behaviour would differ from the patterns I was used to, that is to say, virtually every man that crossed my path, would stand no chance of going beyond the first couple of dates, unaware that they were competing against a perfect ideal that did not exist beyond my own imagination.

I was deliberately boycotting my efforts of turning the page because, deep down, I was not ready to move on. Creating new memories with a new person, who might have made my previous ones fade, meant freeing up space in my heart that was still reserved for Tahir. No matter what someone could say or do, I was feeling completely numb. Those dating failures were to me a reassuring confirmation that I could never again feel the way I had felt towards Tahir. I expected the impossible, finding water in a dry well, and the more I failed to achieve the unrealistic goal I had set for myself, the more I would pursue my relentless quest with even stronger determination. If I could prove to myself that my heart was locked, I would have not risked breaking it ever again.

But you seemed to know my secret too, because, within the first weeks of our relationship, you behaved in a way that got me completely hooked, until, in a relatively short time, I could no longer do without your presence. I had given you all the tools you needed to manipulate my mind and access my battered heart.

At the end of the night, we swapped numbers, and you insisted that we would meet up again the following day.

"Let's take it slow," I told you, finding you a little too pushy.

"I am going to Iran for two weeks on Sunday to celebrate the New Year with my family," you explained. "We only have two days to see each other before I leave."

"Well, we can still talk on the phone while you are away and get to know each other little by little," I rebutted. "There is no need to rush things." But you were very persuasive, as I would learn all too well. You would always have the right answer at the right time, and know exactly which buttons to press to make me give in.

Eventually, we agreed to meet again in town the next day.

I hardly knew you, but I already felt part of your life. From the very first moment, you had opened up to me in a way few men had ever done before, and I found that strange and intriguing in equal measure.

As I was getting ready for our date, scanning my entire wardrobe in an attempt to find an outfit which would look feminine but not too revealing, my babysitter rang to say that she was coming down with the flu and was not well enough to look after Amal that night. I was disappointed at first, and texted one of my mummy friends, Fang, to ask if she could take care of my girl for a couple of hours. But when Fang got back to me saying she was visiting some friends in York, I thought that was a sign that it was better to take things slow and meet again once you had returned from Iran.

"I have been thinking about you all afternoon," you said in your sexy, hypnotising, low voice, when I called you to cancel the date. "We could still meet for a coffee at yours," you suggested casually. "I am very good with children anyway."

That is a terrible idea, my conscience screamed at the top of its lungs in a desperate last-minute attempt to rescue me from a guaranteed crash dive. But I felt as if a spell had been cast over me, making me lose control over my own thoughts. I was completely enchanted and eager to see you again.

I replied hesitantly, "Well, after all, I am nearly ready. I will make dinner and put my daughter to bed. Then we can meet for an hour or so. I don't want to involve her at this stage."

"Fair enough. Shall we say 9 p.m. then?"

I could sense your excitement. You sounded like a little boy who had just been promised a reward for being good. I found that spontaneous side of yours irresistibly cute. Little did I know, at that point, that even those apparently genuine traits of your personality were just a hook to make me fall for you, and let go of any of the defences that would have prevented you from violating my boundaries time and again.

As I opened the door that night and caught a glimpse of your sparkling green eyes, I was taken aback by a violent and visceral emotion pushing me to throw my arms around you and breathe in your woody, manly scent. But I didn't. Instead, I waited for you to make a move. You smiled at me and handed me a present, a box of fancy Swiss chocolates. I gave you a brief hug to thank you for your kind gesture, but you looked embarrassed and uncomfortable, a striking contrast to the overconfident tone you had on the phone just a couple of hours earlier. I was surprised, but I tried not to pay attention to that and showed you to the lounge, while I made coffee in the adjacent kitchen.

As I served you the coffee and sat next to you on the sofa, you told me you were worried sick for your little niece who had been recently diagnosed with an ulcerative disease and had spent the previous few weeks in hospital.

"I rarely drink," you said in a broken voice, "but last night I drank a glass of wine just to cheer up. I was taking a bath and thought … when was the last time I laughed? It's been ages. What if the doctors got it wrong? What if it is something worse?"

That was not how I expected our second date to go, but I was happy that you trusted me enough to share your family woes with me.

"Don't worry, I am here for you," I said, giving you the name of a highly specialised centre I knew in Italy, after you told me that your sister wanted to take her daughter abroad for treatment.

Once you calmed down, we moved on to less serious topics, and I showed you the book we had talked about the night before, which you seemed very eager to read but eventually forgot to take home. The same book I meant to give you on your birthday sometime later.

Then, as I was about to answer one of your many questions, you started playing nervously with the edge of my cardigan, looking distant and distracted. Embarrassed, I stopped talking.

"If I bore you, I think you should go," I said half-jokingly.

"No, you don't!" you replied emphatically. "It's just that you have so much energy, whereas I am a very calm and quiet person …"

"And?" I enquired with a poker face.

"Nothing. I just feel it is a lot to take on," you said in an ice-cold tone.

I did not know what to say.

With just one sentence, you had managed to spoil the magic that I had felt between us, making me feel wrong in the process. I am not sure what exactly offended me so much, if it was your superior attitude, the unconvinced look you had, or the coldness I could sense in your voice. All I know is that I felt deeply humiliated. I just wanted you to leave.

But to my surprise, your face suddenly changed, as if nothing had happened. "It's ten o'clock. Maybe I should leave. So, what do you think? Shall we meet again?" you asked me with a hint of a smile.

I was lost. Trying to figure out what was going on inside your head was a much bigger challenge than I had first thought. But I thrived on challenges. They were the fuel that stimulated my inquisitive and overthinking mind.

"Ask yourself," I replied, slightly annoyed, from the far corner of the sofa where I was curled up hugging my knees, as if defending myself. "You do not seem to like me that much."

"Of course, I want to meet you again," you said, unperturbed.

Then, as I gave you a sceptical look, you came closer to me, our bodies touching for the very first time. You stroked my hair with a gentle movement and kissed me slowly on my neck, sending tingling waves of pleasure throughout my body, as if you had known it more than myself.

What the hell was going on? Just a minute before, you seemed bored and eager to leave, looking at me in a way that had made me feel unwanted. And now, here you were, touching me like nobody else had ever touched me, in such a delicate and tender way that had the power to arouse me and, at the same time, push me to completely abandon myself to your experienced hands, as if my body was no longer mine.

But it was not just my body you took hold of that night as we made love until the early hours, cuddling in bed, and talking intimately with each other, like lovers do.

"You are so different from the girls I have been with," you told me as you ran your fingers down my arms. "You are romantic. You are passionate. And you don't need to get drunk just to be yourself."

I did not know how to take that. Should I have got upset because you were comparing me to your exes just after we had been together? Or should I consider it a clumsy way to compliment me? I decided to go for the latter.

"Whatever happens between us, do not hurt me," I whispered into your ear as the sun started peeking through the windows, the uncontrollable attraction that existed between us slowly leaving room for a hint of rationality.

"I won't," you replied promptly. "I won't because I really like you."

CHAPTER SEVENTEEN

Later that morning, as I woke up alone in bed, I felt on top of the world. It was Saturday, and while I waited for Amal to wake up, I decided to call my sister and share my excitement with her. My entire body still smelled of your perfume, as intense as the emotions that our night together had provoked in me.

After telling her how you had managed to awaken such strong and powerful feelings, even if I had only seen you a couple of times; how deeply connected to you I felt in such an irrational and inexplicable way, my sister cautioned me about falling head over heels without knowing much about you.

"You have just met him. Take it slow," she said with her usually composed, pragmatic attitude. She was my reality check, my alter ego and rational self, my confidante, my partner in crime, and most trusted adviser.

I was a dreamer. An introvert for most of my life, I enjoyed living inside my inner world, a safe haven where truth and imagination converged. She, on the other hand, was a realist. She did not like to dwell on the past, to reflect on her behaviour and others as much as I did, fascinated as I was by the bittersweet inconsistency of human nature. Her world was much more concrete and predictable than mine, and it was a world she was comfortable in.

We were chalk and cheese, so different that I sometimes doubted that we were born out of the same mother. She was four years older than me, and ever since I was a little girl, I always looked up to her as the responsible adult between the two of us, even though, nine times out of ten, I disagreed with her outlook on things, which was much more rational and emotionally detached than mine. Still, I loved to hear her opinion on a given situation. It helped me look at reality from a fresh and unexplored perspective, despite ending up following my instinct.

As a daughter, she was the child most parents would want. She was good, sensible, and reliable, the kind of person someone, including my parents, could turn to for advice, assured that she would present them with a practical solution to any issue they faced. She was a problem solver. I was a troublemaker.

She had taken all the right steps. Got an economics degree from Rome's most prestigious private university, as my father had encouraged her to do, landed a steady job at a state-owned company, met her future husband and lived with him for some time before getting married in church, and had two kids by her late thirties, like many Italian working women did. Her life was unfamiliar with the drama and ups and downs that characterised mine. Unlike my sister, who liked to conform to the majority view, I did not give the answers that my parents—and everybody else—expected from me. But as I grew up, I gradually realised that it was okay because that did not mean I was wrong. I was just different.

Once I understood that, the feeling of guilt for being myself slowly vanished, and I took pride in my renewed sense of self and distinct identity. After all, I could not be responsible for someone's happiness or unhappiness. It was not my job to please everybody and meet their expectations.

I only had one duty in life, to love myself, a task challenging enough to undertake. If I strove to adhere to that single principle, everything else would have fallen into place. I had to stop blaming myself for other people's life choices. I did not need their approval to feel better about my own decisions. At the end of the day, people would always criticise, no matter what.

There would be more "I told you so's" in my life, many more failures and rejections to deal with. But if I took all of them in my stride, I could just focus on living rather than letting myself live. I would finally be free to do whatever I wanted, conscious that I did not need any permission or validation to be happy and enjoy whatever opportunity life would gift me with.

All I needed was a house that smelled of lavender and freshly baked chocolate cookies. A sunset streaked with a multitude of orange and pink shades. The comforting taste of a warm spicy curry on a cold wintry night. The screening of a movie I had been waiting ages to see.

But this hard-won self-awareness was precisely what had attracted you to me in the first place. I was at a stage of my life when I had finally found my inner place, was happy about, and with myself, but also keen to share my happiness with the right person. There was so much light all around me, and my aura was so intense that it could reflect on those nearby.

You sensed that and wanted to take that light, so that it could shine on you instead, drawing me to the dark place at the core of your essence. You were so good at playing with my emotions that you managed to convince me that the crumbs which you would scatter along your way were the best I could ever taste.

"That's true. I hardly know him. But this time, it feels so different," I told my sister. "It's hard to explain. Even just hearing his voice on the phone makes me feel so alive. Sometimes, he even manages to anticipate what I am thinking or am about to say. Isn't that amazing?"

"I am just telling you to be careful, at least until you know exactly what he is after," she said, just before being interrupted by Amal, who was calling me from her bedroom.

"I have to go now. Speak later!" I said and then hung up.

That was the blunt way our conversations would normally end, as someone rang her on the other line, or her kids would fight over the same toy, or we had some work commitment to attend to. But we did not stand on ceremony, so, neither of us would ever get upset if we had to end the call abruptly. It was just the hustle and bustle of day-to-day life.

As soon as I put down the phone, I went straight into Amal's bedroom where I found her with an amused smile, watching two squirrels chase each other on a tree opposite our flat.

"Mummy, look!" Amal screamed, her curious brown eyes filled with excitement.

They stopped for a minute or so to share some acorns they had found at the bottom of the tree.

How cute they are! I thought as I smiled at her. *If only love among humans was as simple as that.*

∞

You love bombed me for the following two weeks, calling me every single night, while, during the day, you would try to make me feel your presence by texting me frequently.

I was very surprised. You were on holiday, visiting your friends and family on a very important occasion, the Iranian New Year, where, as far as I knew, people would gather with their loved ones and spend plenty of time together. But instead, you preferred focusing your attention on someone who, at that point, was virtually a stranger, showering her with compliments and making her feel special. I certainly had not expected that, neither had I asked for it.

He must have a big crush on me, I thought, feeling equally confused and flattered.

"I miss you," you told me on the second night apart, sounding visibly upset.

I laughed, slightly embarrassed.

"Why don't you tell me the same?" you asked.

"How can you miss me? You hardly know me."

"Yes, that's true," you said. "But I really like your personality. You are smart, you are witty, you don't beat about the bush like many girls do."

We would laugh and talk for hours. "You know," you told me one of those nights. "I would normally get bored after a short time when talking to a girl. But with you, I never get bored. You have so many interesting things to say."

At some point during the conversation, you mentioned your ex-girlfriend, an American model you met while holidaying in Greece and had immediately fallen for. "She was so spiritual," you said. "I was there on the beach with my friends, and she said something about how the sound of the waves had the power to calm and slow down one's own thoughts."

Well, that sounds fairly obvious to me, I remember thinking. *Nothing particularly transcendental.*

But I did not want to sound disrespectful towards someone you had loved very much, judging from the sentimental way you talked about her. You told me that, after starting a long-distance relationship, she later moved in with you in Leeds but then, fed up with the uneventful rhythm of Leeds life, she decided to move down to London to continue her modelling career.

"When I visited her in London, she had changed," you said, pointing to that as the reason behind the end of your relationship. "She wanted to stay friends. But I told her I could not be friends with someone I had feelings for."

I totally agreed with you. *How could I relate to anything you would say in such a profound way? So much so that it could have come from my own mouth?* "Yes, I am the same. It is just too painful to be a friend of someone you are in love with," I echoed.

"She kept talking to my sisters in Iran, since she had become close to them, until I got angry and asked her to stop."

I found that a little too harsh, but then I tried to put myself in your shoes, as I always strived to do before judging a situation. In the end, I thought that it must have been hard for you to forget her and did not want to hear about her through your family. It was understandable.

That was what I found peculiar about you. You would often puzzle me with some statement that I would find too extreme, drastic, or just plain weird. Most of the time, however, it would be followed by a much more logical and rational argument, and with such a clarity of mind, that I would completely reconsider my initial impressions and conclude that your explanations and justifications made perfect sense.

But when you mentioned that one morning, as soon as you woke up next to your ex, you told her you had dreamt of sleeping with another woman, I did not know what to make out of it.

"She loved me so much that she got really upset," you smirked, with a hint of smug satisfaction in your voice.

"Well, that's not exactly the nicest thing to say," I said. "Imagine you are with someone you love, and she tells you she dreamt of having sex with someone else. How would you feel?"

"Why? If we get together, we should always be honest with each other and tell each other everything. We should be each other's best friend," you answered, trying to win me over.

Once again, I was at a loss for words. *Can't argue with that*, I thought, even though something did not feel quite right … but I could not pinpoint what that was. Maybe it was the difference between being honest with someone and deliberately hurting someone's feelings for the purely sadistic pleasure of exerting control over them.

You seemed to prove your interest in getting to know me by asking me so many questions about myself and my life, impressing me further when I realised that you remembered all my answers. I was so used to guys who were not great communicators, not to mention good listeners. But with you, I felt immediately understood, as if we were on the same wavelength. What I did not know, though, was that you were trying to gather as much information as possible so that you would have been able to use my weaknesses against me.

I like strong women like you, you texted one day. To which I replied: *Even a strong woman, deep down, dreams of a man who makes her feel safe and protected.*

Yes, that's true, you said. Of course, you knew *that*.

It was exactly this emotional need of mine that you would exploit and turn to your advantage, presenting yourself as a knight in shining armour that would have defended me from any evil anytime I would feel vulnerable. But in reality, the evil you were supposed to fight against was deeply rooted inside of you.

CHAPTER EIGHTEEN

On the fifteenth night, you did not call.

I found it strange, as you had not missed any of our phone dates since you had left. But given that the night before we had already arranged to meet up on the Sunday, the day you would get back from Iran, I thought that you wanted to spend the last night home with your people, rather than on the phone with me. So, I did not get in touch either, even though I had a sinking feeling that I could not really explain.

On Sunday morning, just as I was starting to speculate on the reason behind your prolonged silence, my phone rang. When I read your name on the screen, my heart thumped. That was the effect you had on me every single time we were close to each other.

"Hey, how are you? I have just arrived, but I don't feel very well. I have a terrible cold," you told me as soon as I picked up.

"Aw! Sorry to hear that. It's okay … have a rest. We can meet later, or another time," I said, even though I felt there was more to it you did not want to say.

Just over twenty-four hours before, you were dying to see me again. And now, you sounded very cold and uncomfortable, as if you were struggling to come up with a plausible excuse.

"I wanted to see you, but maybe we should leave it," you added.

"That's fine." I was starting to feel uncomfortable myself.

But then, you changed your mind, possibly sensing my disappointment. "I'll tell you what. I'll pick you up in an hour. Is that okay?"

"Are you sure?" I said, confused. "If you don't feel well enough, let's just cancel."

"No, it's fine," you replied, even though your sceptical tone was giving you away.

"Okay then. I will look after you." I was trying to sound reassuring.

Although your hesitation after we had not seen each other for two full weeks put me off, I accepted to meet up not only because I had been literally counting down the days, but also because I could not wait to look into your eyes and find out whether my doubts were justified.

When, after dropping off Amal at a birthday party, I went back home and found you waiting for me outside the car, that sinking feeling intensified. You looked tired and upset, but I attributed your suffering face to the long flight journey, the jet lag, and the cold. As I got into your car and we drove to your place, I felt tense and uneasy.

How could you look so cold and distant when over the phone you had managed to make me feel your warm presence despite being miles away?

Fair enough, you were sleep-deprived and not in your best shape, but still, I expected that, as soon as you saw me, you would get your energy back. Or at least, that was what I hoped.

Once we reached your place, you left the luggage in the hallway and ushered me in, inviting me to sit on the black leather sofa in the living room, as you made us tea.

While I waited, I took a look around. I was impressed. The house was small but immaculate. Everything was perfectly clean and in the right place, just like I tried to keep mine. Indeed, since my divorce, I had become extremely particular about the house, driven by the belief that tidying up my home—a person's most private and intimate space—would also help me get my life back in order and feel in control. I needed to live in a spotless and perfectly organised environment in order to have clarity of mind, and that was especially important for someone like me whose work was home-based.

Looking after my home helped me feel grounded and focused, just like looking after myself. *Mens sana in corpore sano*, a healthy mind in a healthy body, the Romans used to say. The way I saw it, a tidy house or a well-groomed person expressed a form of love and respect towards oneself as well as to others, so, when I noticed that, just like me, you liked to take good care of your home, as well as yourself, I could perfectly relate to that.

"Wow! What a neat cosy place!" I told you, as I admired the walnut inlaid coffee table and the savannah sunset mural covering the central wall.

"Thanks, I refurbished it and decorated it all by myself," you replied with a proud face.

"Well done. It is very nice. I am terrible at DIY!" I exclaimed, laughing. "Is this where you lived with your ex?" I immediately wished I had bitten my tongue instead of asking such a silly and intrusive question.

"Yes, it is," you replied bluntly.

I was trying to find the right words to ask you where we were going from there, when you suddenly hugged me tightly, once again, sending my heart racing. "Let's talk about that later. I have not even given you a proper hug," you said, before squeezing me even tighter. "I really missed you these days," you added with a sweet smile, as I gently stroked your perfectly trimmed beard and brushed against your chest.

I loved running my fingers down your heavily tattooed arms and back, which were crucial to the masculine, badass image you liked to project. Even though, in my view, those intimidating skin marks were just an armour behind which you tried to hide your fragility.

The tea you made had got cold, but it did not matter. We did not drink it anyway.

Two hours later, as you drove me back home, I was overwhelmed with a whirlwind of conflicting emotions, exacerbated by the fact that, once again, you had gone silent and looked deep in thought. Silence always made me feel uncomfortable, to the point that I would try to fill it in any possible way.

"Who do all those cars parked in your driveway belong to?" I asked innocently. "Are these the ones you repair for work?" I was trying to show interest in your job, but you must have misunderstood the purpose of my question, judging from the unimpressed look you gave me.

"Yes, why do you want to know?" You seemed suspicious, wrongly assuming that I was somehow assessing your financial means.

"No particular reason," I replied. "Just out of curiosity."

That was what, at the beginning, I could not figure out. Every time we were together, I could feel an irresistible attraction and emotional closeness, but accompanied by feelings of inadequacy and frustration, as if whatever I would say or do would be wrong. I was constantly walking on eggshells, trying with all of myself to say and do the right thing, to gain your respect and admiration, to show you that I was worth your time and attention.

But that was only one side of the story. The other side was made of loving and tender moments, of kind gestures, of times you would make me feel like *a girl in a million*, as you would often tell me. You had mastered the carrot and stick approach to such heights of manipulation that I was so entangled in your deceptive love net I was not able to escape. And that was making it much harder to figure out which one of the many sides of your personality, if any, was the most authentic.

Later that day, as I replayed our date in my head, unable to find an answer to the doubts plaguing my mind, I decided to send you a text and explain to you exactly how I felt.

Hi there. I had a good time with you today, but I am at a point of my life when I know exactly what I want and have no time to waste. I had a strange feeling when we were at your place and I am not sure why, but if I see something unclear, I prefer ending things straight away, before they get more serious.

You replied a few minutes later.

Yes, you are right. A relationship cannot only be based on physical attraction. We have great sexual chemistry, but I feel there is something missing in your personality.

I was shocked. Was this the same person who just a few days before had praised me for hours on end for my way of being? And now, you were blaming some flaw in my personality as the reason why things between us could not progress further? No, I could not accept your explanation. It made no sense.

Maybe the date had not gone as we had hoped, maybe the timing was wrong, maybe you were feeling off, maybe it was just a bad day ... maybe ... maybe, but it was not just *my* fault. The eyes cannot lie. I had no doubt about that. And the adoring way you had looked at me as you held me in your arms was no exception.

On an impulse, I picked up the phone and gave you a call. I wanted to hear what you had just written directly from you, in your voice. Maybe, at that point, I would have believed you. Or maybe not.

You replied straight away. "Look, I am really sorry, but I feel there is something missing. I wanted to end it, but now that you've called me, I am no longer sure. If you want, we can still see each other and have a good time," you said, in a calm and detached tone that sent shivers down my spine.

"Is this some kind of bad joke?" I asked you in disbelief. "We meet one night and from the first moment, you sound so keen on me that you make me wonder whether you have been lovestruck. You are so pushy that you don't even give me a chance to reflect on what's going on. You pester me with messages and calls day and night throughout your entire holiday. You talk about us as if we were already a couple. You make plans about things we could do together upon your return. You even insist on joining me on my upcoming work trip and now, out of the blue, you tell me that there is something missing in my personality which, in your own words, was what had attracted you to me in the first place. Make peace with your mind!" I shouted at you outraged, letting out all the anger that had been boiling inside of me since the moment I read your text.

"And how dare you even suggest that we could still hang out together! Who the hell do you think you are?! Do you think I am so desperate that I need you just to have someone to have fun with?!" I went on, screaming even louder. I was fuming. No man had ever insulted me to that extent, and definitely not in the subtle and cunning way you had done.

But why then, even now that you had put your cards on the table, could I not bring myself to hate you? In fact, I wanted you so badly that I could not think about anything else.

"I am being honest with you," you said.

Yes, you had been honest. So, why was I feeling used and manipulated?

This time your tone had completely changed. It was like you had been wearing a mask all along, a mask that had now slipped, revealing your true colours in all their brightness. I don't remember exactly what else you said after that, because I was too shocked by your belittling, patronising, and aggressive attitude to pay attention to the words coming out of your mouth.

"I asked you just one thing, not to hurt me. I opened up to you. I gave you my trust. I told you how much pain I went through with my divorce. I was not ready to go through another heartbreak again. Not now and not this way," I said with a tearful voice. A tiny part of me was still hoping that you would say something that would make me think I had got it wrong, that you were not the nasty person you were showing me, that it had just been a terrible misunderstanding, and I would finally wake up from my bad dream. But you were silent, not showing the slightest hint of empathy.

"I have to go now," you just said and then hung up.

CHAPTER NINETEEN

After that call, I decided to pretend I had never met you.
But that was easier said than done. For some absurd reason, you had got into my head and into my heart from the moment we had exchanged the first few words on that doomed night in mid-March.

I was due to travel on a work trip to Brussels the following week, the same trip you wanted to go on with me.

A change of air will help clear my mind, and, by the time I am back, I will have completely forgotten about him, I thought, as I piled my bag high with tailored dresses, blazers, and suede pumps.

Travelling was the best therapy. Even as a little girl, every time I felt upset or misunderstood, I would fill a backpack with all my favourite clothes and toys and pretend to embark on a solo journey around the world. The urge of exploring new places and discovering new ways of life was in my blood.

As I grew up, that imaginary wandering became a reality. In my reporting roles, I would travel often to places as far as the US, Latin America, and Asia. But when I was not travelling for work, I would still travel inside my mind, devouring books that would take me out of my comfort zone, whose narrators would be people who had first-hand experience of a particular society, and could help me better understand the cultural norms on which it was based from an unbiased perspective.

Often, though, I would travel to escape the ordinary world and reconnect with my inner self. Those were the trips I enjoyed most.

There is no better way to find oneself again than getting lost in an unfamiliar place.

Many years before, as a twenty-something trainee with the European Parliament, I had hopped onto a flight to Barcelona to try and move on from my first painful break-up. He was an aspiring lawyer a few years my senior, who had courted me with love poems, letters, and roses, only to dump me a few weeks later, after a very passionate kiss in front of my fellow trainees and senior colleagues at a charity party I invited him to.

However, something good had come out of it. If it had not been for him, I would not have made that unforgettable four-day trip during which I met a sweet Mexican girl who was studying on a diploma course to become a beauty therapist. Even though the worlds we had come from could not have been more different, we immediately clicked and spent some precious girly time together, sharing details of our love lives as we sunbathed on the Barceloneta beach, going on therapeutic shopping sprees, cooking our own countries' specialties for each other, and chilling out in front of the TV in the evenings with our fellow flatmates. What an amazing breakaway that trip had been! I had lost a lover, but I had found a lifelong friend.

That summer I realised that travelling has the power to heal the soul and bring it back to life, as long as one is willing to embrace the adventure with an open heart and an open mind.

How ironic it was that so many years later, I was finding myself in the same position, that is to say, head over heels for someone whose egocentrism, victimhood, and delusions of grandeur reminded me of that guy.

Would I ever learn?

Maybe, but at least I was neither the first nor the last to repeat the same mistakes over and over again, if falling in love with the wrong person can really be considered such. If philosophers, poets, novelists, and songwriters have dedicated thousands of pieces of work to the allure of toxic love, there must have been a reason. And maybe the reason is that the human mind always desires what it does not have. As simple as that.

Odi et amo. "I hate and I love. Why I do this, perhaps you ask. I know not, but I feel it happening and I am tortured[21]," the Roman poet Catullus had told his lover, distilling in just a few words all the visceral strength of his conflicting feelings.

I can't live with or without you[22], was the band U2's modern twist on the same concept. We were wasting precious energy hating each other, but the truth was we could not be apart.

I got into a taxi and headed to Leeds Station, where I would catch a train to London King's Cross, and from there, board the Eurostar to Brussels. Soon, I felt lightheaded. What was that strong familiar smell? *Bloody Miad*, I could feel your presence even when you were not there. I was trying my best to forget about you, and now, my own senses were teasing me, forcing me to smell your cologne, which the taxi driver had sprayed in massive quantities all over his body.

I tried to distract myself and think about the busy work day ahead. When we arrived at the destination, and I took out my wallet to pay for the ride, I looked at the driver, embarrassed, and timidly asked him that random, completely inappropriate question. "Do you mind telling me the name of the cologne you are wearing?" I said, pretending I liked the fragrance and was looking to buy it for my dad.

"Sure. It's Calvin Klein. *One Summer*," he replied, unperturbed.

"Thank you," I said as I handed him the money and let him keep the change, rushing out of the car, ashamed of the thoughts he could have read in my eyes.

The trip was a disaster. The feeling of humiliation your words had triggered in me was still lingering, and despite trying my best to focus on my work, I could not wait to go back to Leeds and spit all my resentment into your face. I *needed* to see you and tell you what I thought. And this time, you'd better not run away as you had done on the phone.

The next day, as I waited at Brussels Midi Station for the train home, I sent you a brief but straight text: *I will arrive at Leeds Station*

---

[21] "Poem 85," *Carmina* by Roman poet C. Valerius Catullus (c.84–c.54 bc). Translated by Leonard C. Smithers. Perseus Project (1894).

[22] "With or Without You," song by Irish band U2, *The Joshua Tree* (1987).

tonight, just after midnight. No matter how late I reach home, we are still going to meet. We have to talk, and this time, you are going to listen.

A few minutes later, you replied with a voice message, saying that you had been very ill in the previous few days, coughing and generally feeling rundown. How good you were at playing the victim card! But I did not buy it.

I don't care. We are still going to meet, and I am going to tell you all I have to say to your face, was my response.

You replied: *I did not say we cannot meet. Okay. Call me when you arrive and I will meet you at your place.*

I was exhausted after an intense forty-eight hours of back-to-back meetings, but I was also adamant that I would see you that very night. It was written in stone.

Amal was staying with Fang, and I was due to pick her up early in the morning, before dropping her off at school. I could have done with a few hours of peaceful sleep, but I was happy to sacrifice them, if that meant letting out all the negative emotions that I had been harbouring deep inside since we had last seen each other.

When I opened the door and found you in front of me, you gave me an apprehensive stare, as if you were scared that I would slap you in the face that very moment. But revenge was not what I was after. I just wanted to understand how I could have possibly got it so wrong about you. I could not accept you really were the way you were. And in hindsight, that was my greatest mistake: Not believing that someone like you could actually exist. It would have to be some sort of mythological creature because, throughout my life, I had never met someone similar before. But maybe I had just been extremely lucky.

As we sat on the sofa facing each other, I felt as if we were about to start a political debate between two candidates running for presidency. We both wanted to win the race.

I asked you to sit closer to me, as I needed to feel you to make sure that you were real.

But you didn't. "I am fine here," you said.

We would both do the same time and again, distancing ourselves physically to contain the flame that would violently ignite every time our bodies would come into contact. They were shaped in such a way that they seemed to have been created for each other. Every time they would touch, they would click perfectly, like two magnets whose opposite poles are drawn together, but if held the wrong way, they push apart. And just like two magnets, our stored-up energy would decrease when we were close to each other, until we would feel completely empty and drained.

"I don't know what's wrong with me, but I cannot get attached to any girl," you said candidly.

"I don't believe you," I replied. "When we are together, I feel you so deeply. You are one hundred per cent with me ... physically, mentally, and emotionally. I can see that from the way you look at me ... it's like you are giving me all of yourself... but I don't know why you seem to forget that as soon as I am out of sight."

"I always fight against my feelings," you said, as if you were about to surrender.

But then you bounced back. "I try not to get too close to someone because, if I do, I end up hurting them."

At that time, I could not really understand what you meant, but now, it all makes perfect sense: You were hurting others so that they would not be able to hurt you.

"Look, you are a nice girl, but I am just an ordinary guy ... don't take it so hard."

That was another strategy of yours. Trying to show you were much less than the inflated perception you had of yourself to gain people's favour, so that it would be easier for you to use that to your advantage.

When you said you were still feeling unwell and that you had come thinking we would spend "some good time" together rather than arguing for hours, I went ballistic.

You are tired? Poor little thing! What about me? I had a few rough nights because of your despicable behaviour. I have been working out of town for the past two days, but still, I have found the time to see you, in a desperate attempt at rewinding the tape and starting it all over again.

"I am really tired. Shall I sleep here tonight?" you asked me, as if it was the most natural thing in the world.

"Get lost!" I shouted from my bedroom, where I had retreated, no longer interested in making any effort to understand your twisted mind and overcome our misunderstandings.

You were about to leave, but as you reached the doorstep, I stopped you. "Where the hell are you going?" I said, my voice turning desperate.

"You have just asked me to leave," you replied in your typical ice-cold tone.

"And you just leave without even saying bye? If I knew it would have ended up like this, I would have stayed with my friends." I guess I had been over-optimistic.

You made a U-turn and walked towards the bedroom, swearing and shouting along the way. By the time you came closer to me, I had broken down.

You were about to give me a quick peck on the cheek before setting off, as if you were doing me a favour. Then, when you saw me move my head away, you completely lost it.

"You know what? You are bloody crazy. Just leave me alone!" you screamed, absolutely livid.

We were so good at driving each other insane.

You stormed out of the room, scurried through the hallway, and slammed the front door behind you. I could not believe you had done that.

Ten minutes later, I called you. "Did you really leave just like that?" I asked you in disbelief.

"You wanted me to leave."

"Come back," I said. I did not want us to end it like that.

"I am already home now. We will talk later," you told me with a husky voice.

And that's how our tumultuous relationship began.

CHAPTER TWENTY

"You are selfish, self-centred, and —"

"Sexy!" you completed the sentence, smiling with that irresistible impudent look of yours.

"That's not exactly what I was going to say, but I can't argue with that," I replied with a wink. "I seriously hate you. Honestly, I have never met someone as irritating."

"Don't say that otherwise you are going to be in trouble," you threatened, pulling me towards you just as I was about to hit you with a cushion.

"*You* are my sexy little girl," you said, closing your eyes as you kissed me. I always tried hard to resist your advances, fighting against myself to retain control of the situation, as if we were rivals competing against each other.

"What can I do if I can't be next to you without feeling turned on?" you said, giving me your typical tail-between-your-legs look.

"Just keep dreaming," I teased. "You are not going to get any."

"*Yes, I am*," you rebutted, with arrogant self-entitlement. You knew that as soon as you would start stroking me gently all over my body, I would wave the white flag. I just could not help it. You had become my favourite addiction. I could go without seeing you for four, five days at most, but then the first withdrawal symptoms would kick in. I had to see you, to smell you, to touch you to get my energy back. You were the cure and the disease. I needed you like the air I breathed.

"Stop fighting yourself," you would tell me, as you tried to encourage me to completely abandon myself to you. Then, without even giving me a chance to run away, you would lift me off the ground and wrap your arms tightly around mine, as if you wanted to make sure I could not escape. At that point, I would start laughing hysterically and beg you to let me go, but you wouldn't, and I would have no other option than to rest my head on your shoulders and capitulate.

"We must carry on until we get old," you said, in one of those moments of wildness when nothing else existed except our lustful bodies yearning for each other and the sound of our accelerated heartbeats.

Being with you was just like life: tremendously exciting, always unpredictable, often painful.

We would meet at mine or yours every few nights, but I would never be able to anticipate how these encounters would end. Was this what people call a *passionate relationship* when they actually mean hell on Earth? A hell where pain was mixed with pleasure in such an artful way one could not even tell the difference.

Some days, I would feel like I was living a dream. Every single moment would be so perfect that its memory would stay alive in my head until our next rendezvous.

Our bittersweet childhood tales, late-night takeaways, cuddles on the sofa, deep philosophical conversations, silly jokes, and cheeky banter. Your absurd stories about the rich kids of Iran. Your less than amusing accounts of drug abuse, violence, and oppression. Our never-ending hugs that had the power to erase any notion of time and space and delete any worrying thought from the brain.

The cooking and life coaching TV shows you were so passionate about, and the scary movies we would watch curled up together in bed. My excitement as soon as I heard some Spanish tunes on TV. The unfamiliar Persian snacks you would make me taste, and the dinners you would cook for us. Most of the time, they were too salty for my liking, but I would still eat them with great pleasure just because your soft hands made them.

Those hands that you looked after with so much care, slathering them with cream every night before bed.

That sensitive side of yours that would show up, time and again, through some cracks in the wall you had built around yourself that had not been repaired.

Your warm laughter.

On other occasions, it would feel more like a nightmare.

We would start a conversation and suddenly, you would get angry at something I had said, making a mountain out of a molehill. In those moments, you would switch from a caring, funny, and charming person to a nasty, cruel, and spiteful one in a matter of seconds, treating me as if I were your worst enemy, hurting me with harsh words, and distorting reality in order to make me feel guilty.

The first few times this happened, I would desperately try to break the curse that seemed to have been put on you, calmly putting things into perspective to show you it had all been a big misunderstanding. But, as the time went by, I realised that nothing I could have said or done would have brought you back to your senses. You were in a rage, projecting on me all the things you hated about yourself.

All I could do was keep quiet and wait for the storm to pass, even though, every time that happened, a piece of me would break, and the cracks would begin to show on my tired face as much as on my soul.

It took time for me to understand that you did not mean any of the hurtful words that would come out of your mouth, because that anger bottled up inside of you was not directed at me.

We would break up virtually every week and most of the time, for the same reason. I wanted you to give me all the things you could not: commitment, stability, security.

You, on the other hand, wanted to take things as they came, to live in the moment. And this would make me feel frustrated, anxious, and unsettled. But I wanted all of that from you precisely because I knew you could have not given it to me.

We were more alike than one would think. Two free spirits, too independent to let another person control our lives, both averse to long-term plans. I was chasing something impossible because I was too scared to commit to something that was real and possible. You had neither the willingness nor the capacity to commit—to virtually anything. We were both running away from the responsibilities that a mature relationship involves.

But then, a few days after one of our angry break-ups, we would start our infernal dance all over again.

"I can't meet you tonight," I told you one night. "I feel very dizzy and I keep seeing flashing lights. I think I will go to A&E."

"I'll pick you up and take you there."

"Thanks, but it's okay. I'll get a cab. I need to bring Amal with me, and I think it's better you don't meet her."

"Come on! Let me take you. Who is going to look after her while you are inside with the doctor?" As usual, your argument seemed flawless.

"Fair enough. I'll get her ready and I'll meet you downstairs."

I was not sure that introducing you to Amal was a good idea, given that I was still trying to figure out what we were for each other, but I tried to look at things from a more pragmatic perspective. Having you keep an eye on Amal, who most likely would have fallen asleep in the car by the time we reached the hospital, would have been helpful.

Not to mention that I hated hospitals. And it would have been nice to have someone to keep me company while I waited for my turn, like it would have been nice not to have to get back home on my own in the early hours.

"Okay. I'll pick you up in half an hour. See you!" you said before hanging up.

When you saw me coming out of the front gate, carrying Amal in her pushchair as she was about to doze off, you immediately came to the rescue, picking her up and gently placing her in the car seat you had borrowed from a friend, as you buckled her up firmly.

She scrutinised you with a perplexed look, and you gave her the sweetest and warmest smile ever.

"Hello Amal," you said, winking at her before turning towards me. "She is so cute," you whispered, your eyes widened in astonishment.

Only twenty minutes after we reached the hospital, I was called in for my check-up. "Take good care of her," I told you, as I went inside the ward.

"Don't worry, we will be fine," you replied.

When I emerged from the consultation room half an hour later, I saw something that exceeded all of my expectations. You and Amal were deeply engaged in conversation, chatting away like two old friends, laughing and joking together. You had a look of concentration on your face as you listened to her relate stories about her family, the same look that hooked me on the night we met.

"How did it go?" you asked as I sat next to you.

"It's all good. They said you can see those flashing lights when you spend too many hours in front of a computer screen. As for the dizziness, I might just be a little stressed these days ..." I was trying to play down the issue, as I often did when we were together. You were so absorbed in yourself and focused on your own problems that I tried to avoid sharing my worries with you because, on the few occasions I did, you had made me feel as if yours were much more important.

"I am under so much pressure these days. I fight with the garage guys all the time. My mum keeps telling me every single day to find a nice girl and get married. My niece is ill. My sisters are always asking me to do something for them. I have enough. Try to understand," you would tell me every time I would try to figure out what I meant to you.

But what was unreasonable about that? Falling crazily in love with someone and wanting him to be part of your life? I did not believe so. That was the most natural thing in the world. Was it wrong? Was it immature? Was it irresponsible? Maybe it was all of these things. Maybe the most sensible thing to do when you know you hit a brick wall is to give up and move on. And that was what my brain was doing all day long, day after day, telling myself to *let him go* like a mantra.

But the heart has its reasons of which reason knows nothing[23].

"Problems are part of life, Miad. Look at me. I am a single working mother. I live away from my family. I face any hurdles by myself. There are days I feel like giving up. Days I feel so exhausted I just wish I could press a button and stop this crazy ride. But I am here. I am alive. I am free. I have choice, and that itself is a privilege not many people have."

I know. But you are a strong woman, you would say, as if that would not give me the right to complain.

That's just nonsense. Life is what you make it. People are not born strong or weak. They become what they choose to be, I would rebut.

---

[23] A quote by French mathematician and philosopher Blaise Pascal (1623-1662).

You knew I was right, and that was what frustrated you most. Knowing that, in front of you, there was someone who kept challenging your ever-changing ideas and beliefs, a sort of alter ego from whom it would have been hard to run away, branded as she was on your skin just like your intimidating tattoos. She was the truth you could not face, the reflection you could not see, she was everything you were not, and yet, everything you wished you could be. And that thought was driving you insane.

You strived to be a nice person, but your lack of empathy kept giving you away. How could you want someone who was exposing all the things you hated so much about yourself? Someone forcing you to face the demons that you had been carefully hiding from the rest of the world most of your life, burying them deep in the ground and fabricating a fake persona that was much more confident, stronger, and tougher than your true self?

Who is this girl that seems to be perfectly in touch with her inner being, to the point that she is not afraid of expressing her own feelings time and again, to break down my defences, in such a spontaneous and natural way that always leaves me speechless? you would think.

We were talking two different languages. You were so used to calculating every step you would make and every word you would say that you were terrified at the thought of losing control. And that is why you would run as fast as you could every time my heart would speak to you. Because you hated feeling scared and vulnerable.

After all, that is how you felt that time your father had taken you climbing on the Tochal mountains, just outside Tehran.

You must have been six, seven at most, when, once you reached the peak, you hugged your dad tightly, in awe of the breathtaking view one could enjoy from the top.

"What are you doing? Are you a little girl or what? A real man does not show affection," your father had scolded you with a stern look. Immediately, you let go of him, feeling deeply ashamed and confused.

Why was it so wrong for a little kid to hug his daddy?

You were struggling to find the answer, but as you grew older, that feeling of shame and humiliation you had experienced that day kept haunting you until your mind silenced that question. *Feelings make you weak. And nobody respects someone who is weak. But if I suppress my feelings, I can rule the world, and nobody will ever humiliate me and disrespect me again,* it told you.

"I really like your friend. He is *so* funny!" Amal said as I put her to bed and tucked in her blankets, once we got back home from the hospital.

I gave her a bittersweet smile. That was what everybody would have thought if they had met you for the first time. You were Prince Charming. But I would have never let you manipulate her as you had done with me. There were very few certainties in my life. But this was one of them.

CHAPTER TWENTY-ONE

At last, summer came, bringing along a wave of new life goals and revived determination.

After many months of unsuccessful mortgage hunting, at the beginning of the year, I had managed to secure a loan from one of the high street lenders, which had turned my dream of getting on the property ladder into a reality.

It took me a few good months to find the right place for our little family, but when I was finally handed the keys to my new flat, in a leafy residential area in the north of Leeds, I knew that it was the home I had been looking for.

Even though there was still so much to do—painting, redecorating, lighting, floor fitting—it was great to know that, from that moment on, there was a place somewhere in the world that I could call mine, a place that I could not wait to fill with love and happy memories, with warmth and laughter, mirrors, pictures, and souvenirs that would remind me of all the amazing trips I would take around the world.

I would always feel nervous when embarking on a long-haul journey due to my fear of flying, which, for a natural globetrotter like myself, was the biggest paradox ever. But control freak that I was, the idea of spending ten to fifteen hours on a plane, at the mercy of hostile atmospheric conditions, would give me shivers of sheer panic, to the point that I would not be able to relax until I had reached my destination.

During those moments, when the plane would lurch from side to side, I would look at my fellow passengers, who seemed able to engage in funny conversations, enjoy their meals. and watch a movie, while in my anxious mind, catastrophe was imminent. Their nonchalance perplexed me.

It's funny how humans only seem to realise how privileged they are once they may be about to lose that privilege. The only thing that would help me rationalise the situation was thinking about everything I had in my life and make a mental note of all the plans that were still pending. *Riding through the Argentinian Pampas. Attending an intensive flamenco course at a professional dance school in Seville. Writing a book. Taking a tour of Japan during the cherry blossom season. Opening an Arabian tea room in the Leeds student area. Forgetting Miad* … yes, that was the most challenging project of all, but I was determined to go through with it. Well, my brain was.

After all, the one thing you can give people you care about is time. Time to let go, to reflect, and to realise how it feels when you will no longer be there to fill that void. All those moments that are more meaningful and intense than the thousand days that go by one after another, all looking the same. Because at the end of the day, what happens is what is meant to happen. And when you find yourself having to explain things that cannot be rationally explained, it is time to smile, walk away, and just carry on.

But where to start?

You were that dreamy smile that starts from within without you even realising it. That takes you aback in the least expected moments, when you are queuing at the supermarket, causing people around you to giggle. While you are trying to focus on a story you have been chasing for ages.

Like a sudden downpour that catches you unprepared when you have just set out for your morning run.

"Why are you smiling, mum? Because I told you that today at school Emma ripped up my drawing? That's not funny," Amal told me off on one such occasion.

"No, sweetie. I just remembered something silly that made me smile," I replied as I was thrown back into reality.

But something had changed inside me since I had received some news that had made me feel hopeless for the very first time in my life.

The flashing lights that had pushed me to rush to the hospital that night had become a recurring phenomenon. After consulting an ophthalmologist for a second opinion, I was told that I was suffering from a chronic eye condition that had resulted in some irreversible retinal damage, and could have caused my vision to deteriorate over time.

When I listened to him explain the situation in a clear and coherent way that left no room for doubt, I felt my whole body shake. I was in utter shock. The idea that I could gradually lose my sight, that all the things I was taking for granted were no longer a certainty, that I would not be able to see Amal's cheeky eyes, to watch her slim, childish body slowly develop into that of a grown-up lady, to enjoy sunsets and full moons, waves crashing onto the shore and mountains covered in snow, blue skies and pink blossoms, ancient cathedrals and towering skyscrapers ... to no longer distinguish the many shades of colour that make the world such a unique place, was a petrifying thought.

But after a few agonising weeks during which I tried to make sense of such a discovery, I started looking at the situation under a different light. That is to say, as an opportunity to live fully in the present and stop wasting my time worrying about anything that may or may not have happened.

I swore to myself that, from that moment onward, I would seize any opportunity without overthinking it. I would spend every waking moment doing the things I enjoyed. I would start working on those projects hidden somewhere inside a drawer. I would pluck up the courage to fly to the end of the world, even if inside me I would be dying to get off the plane. I would stop finding excuses to procrastinate. I would take over the world and have the best time of my life.

And that also meant to stop chasing impossible stories. Like the one between me and you.

I was hoping the fact that Tahir had asked me to accompany Amal on her first visit to her Omani family since we had left Muscat one and a half years before would help me detach myself physically and emotionally.

"Don't worry. Just take a break and come to Oman for a few weeks. Pray to God and everything will be fine, 'Insha'Allah," Tahir had suggested when I had broken the bad news to him.

Despite our painful split, he was still my best friend, a reliable yet distant presence in my life which I knew I could count on at any time.

I admired his relentless faith. *How could he blindly trust something that was outside of his control?* Maybe precisely because it was beyond human understanding. He had an unwavering belief that everything would turn out well. And if it did not turn out as hoped, what was the point in worrying about it anyway?

There was no point indeed.

It was strange to go back to Oman, a country that would always hold a special place in my heart, now that we were no longer together. To see his family, to smell scents, and to taste dishes that were all too painfully familiar and that I had missed every day since I had left Muscat. Above all, it was strange to spend time again as a family.

During our four-week stay, Tahir tried his best to make our time as enjoyable as possible, displaying all the warm sense of hospitality that is deeply entrenched in Omani culture.

He took us on a 4x4 road trip across northeast Oman, up to the port city of Sur, the shipbuilding capital of the Ash Sharqiyah South Governorate, whose peaceful waterfront is dotted with traditional wooden vessels, seagulls, and watchtowers made out of sandstone.

On the way, we stopped at Hawiyyat Najm—the falling star—an impressive natural limestone sinkhole filled with dazzling turquoise water, squeezed between the mountains and the sea, and which, as a local legend goes, was created by a meteorite.

As I dipped into the crystalline waters, enjoying the mesmerising surroundings, I took in the breathtaking beauty of the place, carefully recording every little detail in my mind, as if I was taking hundreds of snapshots that would allow me to keep those moments as vivid as possible for a long time to come.

A splashing sound distracted me from my thoughts, and as I looked up, I felt streaks of water dripping down my face. I gave Tahir a *don't you dare* look, but he seemed unperturbed and started splashing me even harder. *It is time to retaliate*, I thought, as I pushed the water in his direction with all the strength I had, while Amal looked over amused. *How could it feel so perfect?*

It seemed that now that we no longer had a reason to fight, now that there were no words left unsaid between us, all the tension that had been building up in the last few years of our marriage had evaporated and drifted away, and we were just free to be ourselves, without feeling any pressure to meet each other's expectations.

While I watched Tahir and Amal from a distance as they thoroughly scanned Ras Al Hadd's sandy beach in search of seashells, I wondered whether it was worth going against everything and everybody to be together. And the truth is, I did not have an answer.

We had decided to spend a couple of days at the famous beach resort to watch the giant green turtles bury their eggs on the shore at night before returning to the sea.

"Mummy! Look what we found! A *gigantic* shell," Amal screamed excitedly as she ran towards me, pointing at her peculiar discovery.

"Wow! That's the biggest shell I have ever seen. Well done, my love," I said as I squeezed her tightly.

"Actually ... daddy found it! Isn't he a star?" she exulted proudly.

"Of course, he is. He is the best dad in the whole entire universe," I stated, winking at Tahir.

She was the answer.

∞

The phone rang as I was busy unpacking. I picked up without even paying attention to the number on the screen.

I had deleted your number before leaving for Oman, so when I heard your croaky voice on the other end of the line, I startled.

"I missed you a lot," I heard the distant voice say. "I have been thinking to call you for the past few days ..."

My response, though, was not as warm and affectionate as you expected. The memory of our last brutal fight was still too fresh in my head to be erased by a few sweet words.

I curse the day I met you! You had shouted at the top of your lungs, as you urged me to get out of your life once and for all, punching the door for good measure.

How could I love someone who could make me feel so vulnerable?

"I am sorry for what happened," you said. "I should not have said those horrible things. It's just that sometimes I say things I don't mean. I must have taken after my father. But I don't want to be like him. I want to be better."

When we were in the middle of an argument, your tongue would become sharper than a knife. That was nothing new. What was new, though, was my restored confidence. I was no longer willing to put up with your lame excuses.

"What do you want, Miad? I've had enough. I am tired of fighting. We are just not good for each other. Let's face up to reality," I said with a resigned sigh.

"Please. I want to see you. I'll be back from Iran next week if the protests stop by then."

"Bloody hell! I've just heard that on the news. Is your family all right?"

"Things are pretty bad here. I can't even talk about it. The regime is shutting down the Internet, cracking down on demonstrators ... I only managed to call you because my friend helped me connect to a VPN."

The thought that something could have happened to you had thrown me into a state of panic. "Please be careful," was all I could say.

"Don't worry. I am going to call you as soon as I am back," you said, sensing that my defences were slowly crumbling.

"I don't think it is a good idea."

"I am going to call you anyway!" you teased me with your typical cocky demeanour.

And I am not going to pick up, I was about to reply, playing my trump card, when the line abruptly cut off.

And I wished that the insane, unreasonable, and obscure bond that had united us from day one could have been severed as easily as that.

CHAPTER TWENTY-TWO

"Why is he behaving like this *now*?" I asked Fang one afternoon when we had gathered at my place for our weekly playdate with the kids.

"Because he cares about you," she replied matter-of-factly, as if that was a truth too obvious to be ignored.

"Maybe, but I find it strange. He seems to have turned into the perfect boyfriend overnight," I muttered, as I raised the cup of green tea that had now got cold to my mouth.

I admired Fang's pragmatism, her ability to analyse any situation in a detached and composed way, just like my sister could do.

I, on the other hand, took everything to heart.

As a female born under China's one-child policy, she had managed to escape death thanks to her mother, who had eluded the surveillance of the hospital staff that was due to perform an abortion on her, because her husband, a high-ranking official in the Communist party, already had a son from a previous marriage.

Her mother, though, fled through the window, an act of rebellion that cost her husband everything: his face, his job, his political career, and his financial security. Fang was raised by her maternal grandma in a small village near Beijing, while her parents lived in the city with her half-brother, who, in Fang's words, was much more talented, smarter, and more charming than she was. That was what everybody had told her since she was a little child, to the point that she had convinced herself of that. The feeling of rejection she had experienced from the moment she had come into the world, along with the sense of guilt that her family had instilled in her for having crushed her father's ambitions with her sheer existence, had taken a toll on her, making her feel vulnerable and insecure.

She had been scarred for life.

In a defensive move, she decided to shut the world out and stop talking. She felt as if whatever she would say, would not matter anyway. All her family's attention was focused on her brother.

"I was the ugly duckling. And that's how I still feel," she had confessed to me once, as we chilled out on the sofa eating takeaway pizza, our energy drained by a busy afternoon with the kids, constantly acting as referees so they would stop fighting.

"How can you say that? You are stunning, you are intelligent, you are fun and … you are the best yoga teacher I have ever had!"

But she did not seem to believe me.

That is the common thread that seems to unite most women, regardless of their nationality, social status, or cultural background— our innate insecurity. No matter how often people praise us for our achievements and how proud we feel about them. No matter how much strength we show to the rest of the world, when we are alone with ourselves in front of a mirror, we still hear that disapproving voice telling us off as if we were misbehaving children. *You are not good enough*.

It was a voice that I myself had been struggling to ignore since my early teens. And believe it or not, that voice could be extremely convincing. Time and again, it had pushed me into the arms of unaffectionate individuals. It had persuaded me that I did not deserve to be loved as much as anybody else.

Since you had come back from Iran, you seemed a different person.

For a start, you were much more present in my day-to-day life. Even when we were not meeting up, we would still speak every day on the phone, listening to each other as we shared some funny episode that had occurred at work, or vented about the intrusiveness of our respective families.

You would shower us with attention, surprises, and gifts, and spend afternoons at my flat when we played board games with Amal, or you carried out some DIY job that had been on my to-do list for ages and I kept procrastinating.

"I got Amal two goldfish," you told me one day as soon as I picked up the phone.

I smiled. Just a couple of days before, I had mentioned that Amal had asked me to get her a little sister, as if that were the easiest thing in the world.

"Babies don't come just like that," I attempted to explain to her, trying to hide my embarrassment. "You need two people to make a baby, and daddy and I ..."

I had prepared for that moment, devouring dozens of child psychology books to make sure that I would say the right words. When the time came however, my mind went completely blank. *Always tell the truth to your child*, was the only teaching I could remember. And I was adamant to stick to that. But just as I was about to explain to Amal in a tactful yet honest way that her daddy and I were no longer an item and would never be back together, she anticipated my words, displaying a healthy dose of pragmatism and common sense which seemed atypical of a five-year-old.

"I know you and daddy are no longer together. But he could still be a daddy to your baby," she replied, unperturbed, before adding: "Fair enough. If I can't have a sister, what about a goldfish?"

I laughed and wondered why, as we grow up, we tend to lose the ability to adapt to life circumstances and make the most of them, a gift most of us are born with.

When you grow up, you will understand, my mum would often tell me when, rebellious child that I was, I would question her authority and challenge her steadfast convictions. But is it truly the case? Or is it rather that, as children, we have already got our priorities right, capturing the true essence of life through our pure and untainted lenses, and as we grow up, we tend to lose that carefree approach, busy as we are chasing fleeting illusions that are disguised as vital needs?

"These goldfish are just like babies. You need to give them fresh water, feed them, and take care of them so that they can grow strong and healthy," you told Amal as you thoroughly scrubbed the fish tank that would be home to her new pets.

Every time I saw how patient and devoted you were in her presence, I wondered why you could not be like that the rest of the time. Maybe it was because she appealed to that part of you that had never grown out of your childhood insecurities.

"We will call them Goldie and Whitie," Amal announced, beaming with excitement. And day after day, month after month, year after year, Goldie and Whitie were hanging in there, playing and putting up with each other in the fish tank that Amal had decorated with a fluorescent bridge ornament, colourful gravel, and crystal stones, and which we had placed on the kitchen windowsill. They were getting bigger and stronger as the time went by, living proof of the nurturing power of love.

∞

It was a mild evening in late October when you broke the news. The air smelled of burnt logs and roasted chestnuts, and I had just arrived home after enjoying a deep-tissue massage and a facial at my favourite Thai beauty parlour. Every week, I would strive to allocate a few hours to my wellbeing—whether that meant sweating it out in the local gym, going for a walk into town and splashing out on a few new outfits, or giving myself a complete makeover, did not really matter. What mattered was that this well-deserved me-time helped keep me grounded and reconnect with the world.

That is how I felt when I crossed the doorstep and took off my shoes, relaxed and full of energy. I undressed and got ready for a hot bubble bath, accompanied by some chill-out tunes. Amal was having a sleepover at Fang's place that night. After changing into my pyjamas, I made myself a sandwich and a cup of tea, and went straight to bed, looking forward to some reading and an early night. But just as I started to feel sleepy, the phone rang.

"I messed it up big time. Can we meet up?" you told me with a panicky voice, cutting to the chase.

Half an hour later, I ushered you into the lounge, still wearing my PJs along with a puzzled look. As we sat opposite each other on the sofa, I scanned you from top to bottom to try and figure out what was troubling you so deeply at that time of the night. Your anguished face did not look very promising, but I was so used to your sudden mood swings and the dramatic way you would exaggerate even the most trivial issues, that I retained my self-control while trying to calm you down.

"What happened? Did you kill someone?" I asked, hoping that my surreal question would help ease the tension, rather than fearing an affirmative answer.

"I didn't. But I have done something really stupid. I am so ashamed of myself. I could not bring myself to tell anybody." The frown on your face had grown bigger, and I wondered whether you had withheld some information about your life I should have been aware of.

"Just tell me. There is a solution to any problem in life except death," I said, glad that, one more time, you felt comfortable enough to share your most hidden secrets with me.

"Last night, I was bored at home and started playing some games on my laptop. Business is slow these days, so I thought that if I could get some extra cash online, I would have enough for our trip to Brazil," you explained in such a way that would prevent you from taking full responsibility for your actions, as was always the case.

I still was not quite sure what you were going on about, so I asked you for clarification, praying that my worst fears would not materialise. "What do you mean? How could you make money that way?"

My brain, however, was already anticipating what you were going to say.

"I bet online. And lost 3,000 pounds in just an hour," you confessed, burying your face in your hands.

We were due to fly to São Paulo just a few days later. I had been asked to attend a conference there, and when you heard that, you had enthusiastically offered to accompany me on the trip.

"What are you going to do there all alone? It is such a long journey and not the safest place in the world. I am going to be your bodyguard!" you had joked cheekily.

It was supposed to be our first trip together. An entire week for the two of us, where we could finally have a chance to truly get to know each other. I was nervous and excited at the idea of waking up in bed with you for seven consecutive days, to eat together, shop together, wander around the city, and do any of the things that people normally do when they are on holiday as a couple.

But your unwarranted surprise had left me speechless. I could put up with your difficult personality, your fear of commitment ... even with your OCD traits, but, as madly in love as I was, I was not sure I could accept to be with someone with a gambling addiction. Because even if you were not explicitly acknowledging that, my sixth sense was telling me that it was not the first time you had lost money to gambling, and, most likely, it would have not been the last.

And a woman's intuition rarely fails, especially when she is so emotionally connected to someone.

"I went to the casino a few times when I was younger, but I never lost that much," you eventually admitted, feeling the urge to let out all your growing frustration.

I was furious, but I knew that adding fuel to the fire was not going to help in any way.

"You're right. You really messed it up, but still, it is not the end of the world. Money comes and goes. People rack up thousands of pounds in debt and, most of the time, manage to pay it off. Just pretend you took out a loan and work hard to repay it. All that matters is that you learn from your mistake and never do it again," I said, hoping that my sermon would be enough to bring you back to your senses.

"I know it could be much worse, but I can't help but feel so ashamed."

"Don't think that way. Let it go. We are going away next week. Let's just take it easy, enjoy our time, and, once we get back, you'll try to recover the money little by little."

It was ironic that, even at a time when you were one hundred per cent to blame for your wrongdoing, you had managed to lay part of the blame on me, as if, had you not planned to accompany me on my trip abroad, you would have not gambled online to raise money for your travel expenses.

∞

The week went much better than I expected. There were of course some ups and downs, as was typical of our relationship. Like when, while we were dining and laughing together in the hotel restaurant on our second night in São Paulo, you got livid with jealousy as you accused me of flirting with a Spanish chap in his fifties who was sitting alone at the table next to ours.

He looked very lonely and miserable, and keen to talk to a fellow human being. Indeed, during dinner, he had made at least three attempts at starting a conversation with us after noticing that we spoke English.

At first, I just smiled, slightly annoyed with his intrusive ways, but when I saw that he would not give up, I immediately felt sorry for him, as anybody with a little bit of empathy could have sensed that his apparent overfriendliness was a clumsy attempt at hiding a painful story.

He told us that he was a lecturer in Hispanic Studies at a private university in Chicago and that he had travelled to Brazil a few times to visit some of his students. How many times he must have rehearsed that line!

Enough to believe his own lies.

But that is what many of us do throughout our life. We build a castle of narcotising illusions that will help us avoid facing the truth. Because no matter how hard we try to sugar-coat it, it will still hurt. But what we often fail to realise is that a life based on lies hurts much more.

We moved on, talking about Spanish literature and music, which I was very fond of.

"Have you been to the Sacromonte quarter in Granada? It is the best place to enjoy an authentic flamenco show," our newly acquired friend Pablo had enquired after sharing my passion for the traditional dance.

"Yes, I have been to Granada, indeed. *Give him alms, woman, as there is nothing worse than being blind in Granada*[24]," I replied, reciting a famous quote about the city.

---

[24] Quote by Mexican poet Francisco Asís de Icaza (1863–1925).

As I looked up, I noticed you were staring at me with a cross expression. It did not even enter my mind that your bad temper was due to the fact that I was simply trying to be nice to a lonely man who was much older than me.

"Let's go," you repeated a few times, as Pablo had started debating the striking social inequalities of Latin American countries.

I winked at you and nodded my head, lightly tilting it towards the guy, to signal that I was waiting for him to finish the sentence before wishing him a good night.

But you could not contain your anger. "We must go," you interrupted him bluntly, as you grabbed me by the arm. "What's wrong with you?" you finally exploded as we walked back to the room.

"What do you mean?" I asked, confused. "He is clearly upset over something. I was just trying to be kind to him. That's all. Anybody that crosses your path may have an interesting story to tell you, if you care enough to listen."

"I know, but he was rude. Interfering in our conversation like that? He should have respected that you were with me!" you said, stressing the last two words. You sounded like a spoiled little boy who does not want to share his favourite toy with any other kid. "*You are too friendly with people.*"

What were you hinting at?

"I just like talking to people. Connecting with them. That's my way of being. If you see malice wherever you look, that's not my problem."

"I'll tell you what. I'll go back to the restaurant and have a beer. I don't feel like going to bed now. I'll be back in half an hour or so," you said, closing the door behind you.

CHAPTER TWENTY-THREE

"You were right," you said when you re-emerged two hours later in a cheerful mood, shortly after I had texted you to make sure you had not banged your head against a wall or chatted up some girl out of revenge.

But apparently, you had done none of that. Instead, you had spent the rest of the evening deeply engaged in a man-to-man conversation with Pablo.

"I told him I did not like his behaviour. That you are not my wife but still, he had been quite disrespectful."

I couldn't believe my ears. I felt so embarrassed. "Did you really tell him *that*?" I asked you, incredulous.

"Yes. And he apologised. He also told me he is gay."

"What? But didn't he say he had divorced his wife of thirty years?"

"Yes, but after that, he fell in love with one of his students, a guy from Rio de Janeiro. They had a relationship, but, when the guy finished his course, he returned to Brazil. Pablo could not stop thinking about him, so he decided to travel to Rio to meet him. That's the *real* reason why he is here."

"Why is he in São Paulo then, rather than with his lover?"

"Because when he finally met him and stayed at his place, he found an opened pack of condoms in his drawer, and from there, he understood that they were not in an exclusive relationship as he had first thought. The guy then told him he was not in love with him, and Pablo was too devastated to fly back home. He took the first flight to São Paulo hoping that getting lost in an unknown city would help him forget about him, but it didn't. He still feels heartbroken."

Wow! From the first moment I had seen him, I had felt that his sad eyes hid some precious secret, but that was far beyond what I had imagined. Still, I could deeply relate to his feelings, such is the universal language of love. The powerful longing for someone who had managed to shake your most unwavering certainties, to touch your soul and grab hold of it, leaving behind a void too great to fill. I knew that feeling far too well. In fact, that's exactly how I felt every time we would split up.

Still, I was surprised that he had opened up to you in such an intimate way, especially considering that you had even told him off for talking to your girlfriend and that, in all fairness, you were not the most empathetic and understanding person one could ever come across. But after all, it is much easier and liberating to share your personal woes and frustrations with a complete stranger whom you may never see again, than with a close friend, as proved by the thousands of people who ask for advice about their life problems on social media these days, and by the thousands of impromptu agony aunts who are more than happy to offer such advice.

"He saw I had been frank with him, so he did the same with me. I am always honest with people even if they may get offended," you said with a hint of pride in your voice. "If you are honest with them, they will be honest with you."

Every time you would start lecturing me about morals and what a nice person you were, I would shut my ears. I believed there were two types of nice people in the world—those who were genuinely nice, and those who were nice to gain others' approval and support, and eventually, exert control over them.

And I had started suspecting you were one of the latter.

∞

The following morning, when I bumped into Pablo at breakfast, we exchanged a look of tacit understanding, as if we were telling each other, *I know your secret and you know mine.* We had both fallen in love with the wrong person.

And further proof of that was that, only a few hours after our silly argument about my supposed flirtatiousness, your paranoid thoughts resurfaced when you accused me once again of disrespecting you in public.

I was sitting at a table alone, waiting for you to join me for breakfast while you were deciding which outfit to wear for the occasion. I found it amusing that you were the only man I had been with that could take longer than me to get ready. But for a narcissist like yourself, that was hardly surprising.

As I started drinking my coffee, a local reporter, who was attending the same conference as me, spotted the press badge that I had placed on the six-seater table and asked me if he could sit next to me. Shortly after, two lawyers and a government official, who were also among the conference attendees, joined in.

I thought that was the perfect chance to make some new contacts. After all, that was the main reason why I was there in the first place: networking.

As we started chatting about work-related topics, which most people would have found too intense for an early morning conversation, you swaggered into the restaurant, looking as handsome as ever. But shortly after taking the seat opposite mine, you told me you would move to another table, looking visibly uncomfortable, as I exchanged business cards with my new acquaintances.

"I can't believe you did it again," you hissed when I reached your table to wish you a good day before the conference started. I couldn't believe it either. How could you be so deeply insecure that you would see any other male as a threat to your own inflated ego?

"What are you talking about? I was just carrying out my job." I was angry at myself for even feeling the need to give you explanations.

"Fair enough. I did not know that carrying out your job implied completely ignoring me when we were supposed to have breakfast together."

You could go from behaving in an extremely rational and mature way to acting out as a five-year-old in a matter of seconds. But even though you rarely admitted your mistakes, you were still able to apologise for them in a clumsy and implicit way that I found irresistibly cute. And that was exactly what you were trying to do this time. I just smiled, gave you a kiss, and carried on with the busy day ahead, unwilling to give in to your childish tantrums.

∞

The taxi driver we had hired for the day was speeding so much that I was scared of being catapulted out of the window at any time. But you did not seem particularly worried. In fact, appearing fearless and tough at all times was key to your self-serving fight against anything and anybody that would cast doubts over your distorted perception of reality.

Still, as soon as you realised that I was getting nervous, you asked the driver to slow down, with the same protective attitude that you had with Amal every time you would drive us around, repeatedly checking on her through the front mirror to make sure she was okay, and that her seat belt was still tightly in place despite the bumps on the road.

Then, as if it were the most natural thing in the world, you rested your head on my lap.

I felt embarrassed. I was not used to such public displays of affection, which used to make Tahir so uncomfortable.

The taxi driver winked at me through the front mirror, as we drove past Paraisópolis, São Paulo's second-largest slum neighbourhood, adjacent to the wealthy district of Morumbi, a painful reminder of the country's striking rich and poor divide which seems to be widening year after year.

I gently stroked your shiny dark hair and watched you as you lay there with your eyes closed, holding tightly onto my knees and looking as innocent and vulnerable as a baby. I could not help but feel a pang of tenderness and sympathy for your damaged soul.

∞

"I was actually thinking to buy you a perfume, but then I remembered what a friend recently told me," you said as I opened a bag containing a set of fancy toiletries, a card, and a pot of chrysanthemums.

We had returned from Brazil just on time for my birthday, which I was planning to celebrate by throwing a house party with my closest friends. A party you had also been invited to, but after some back-and-forth, you had eventually decided not to attend because your mum had just come over from Iran, and you had to spend the evening with her. Although I knew what that actually meant—you were not ready to go official and be introduced to my friends as my boyfriend.

"He said that, if someone gifts you with a perfume, you are doomed to separate from that person. I don't really believe it but still ..."

I did not believe it either. I had never been particularly superstitious, but that got me thinking. Tahir often bought me perfumes.

"Well ... I am not sure what's worse, to be honest. Whether we separate because of a silly superstition or because I am going to kill you right now since, on my birthday, you dared to give me a pot of flowers that in Italy are reserved for dead people," I said, bursting into uncontrollable laughter.

"Really?"

"Yes. It is no coincidence they call it *the flower of the dead*. They are traditionally used in funerals and brought to dead people when you visit them in the cemetery."

I could not help but notice the irony of the situation. It was as if your subconscious had been attracted by that flower because that was how you felt deep inside your soul—empty and numb, just like death. And even on a festive day such as the anniversary of my birth, that was all you could offer me.

But what really struck me was that you did not want to risk losing me, not even due to a ridiculous superstition.

You wouldn't anyway, you knew that all too well. I was trapped inside of you as you were inside of me.

CHAPTER TWENTY-FOUR

You did it again. This time, though, the stakes were much higher. You had blown 17,000 pounds, a person's annual salary, in one single night.

"What's wrong with you?" I shouted at the top of my lungs when, moments after I had got into your car, you confessed that you had used the money that a friend of yours had given you, to fund your gambling addiction.

It was a gloomy Saturday morning. You were driving me back home from a place you knew in the Elland Road industrial estate, where you had offered to take me when I told you I was looking to decorate my kitchen walls with tiles.

"I don't know," you said, sighing resignedly.

I was out of my mind and unleashed all my frustration, launching into a tirade against your lack of respect for yourself and others.

"I really don't get it. You are such an intelligent person. How could you have so little self-esteem and self-love to destroy yourself like that? And if you really want to screw up, take responsibility for that. Bet as much as you want with your own money. Don't play with other people's lives! That is such an irresponsible and despicable behaviour. Don't you have any morals? Don't you feel any guilt or remorse?"

I could no longer control myself. You had tested me too many times.

"I know. And I feel really terrible. I feel like killing myself," you muttered in a faint voice.

I had read somewhere that narcissists employ suicide threats as a tactic to get people's attention and force them into doing what they want, and it was not the first time you had revealed to me that you had suicidal thoughts. But not once had I felt you would act upon them. This time, however, I was seriously worried.

"Don't even dare say that," I scolded you, feeling hopeless. And then yelled: "*You must stop playing the victim, Miad.*"

I did not want to empathise with you. Not only because I couldn't, as I was feeling completely drained on a mental and emotional level. But also because I knew that would have been totally counterproductive. I wanted to splash a glass of cold and bitter truth onto your face, hoping that you would finally wake up to reality.

"You must stop seeing the world as a place full of bad people who want to mess with you. Stop laying the blame on them and take control of your life for God's sake!" I ranted on. "You are in a big mess, that's true. But maybe that's exactly what you needed to finally open your eyes and make a change. Everybody can do that, as long as they want to. All you need is some willpower. Sometimes though, you also need the support of a professional to help you achieve that goal."

Although the shocking gravity of the situation had made me feel powerless and out of control, I still managed to reconnect with my rational self and suggested that you take up a job that would provide you with a steady income until you had cleared your debts.

"Why don't you get a taxi license? You love cars and are very good at driving. And it would give you enough flexibility to carry on with the garage as a side business."

"Yes, that's a good idea. I am going to look into that," you replied, just before adding, without a hint of emotion: "You know … I was thinking we should stop seeing each other."

"What?"

"Yes, I have been thinking that as soon as I opened my eyes this morning. I need to focus on myself, work hard day and night, and sort out my life."

I was gutted. You kept screwing up your life, and the first thing that had come to your mind was that, in order to fix it, you had to get rid of the only person who truly cared about you and wanted to help you, driven by a saviour complex which many of us suffer from at some point in our lives.

Overnight, I had turned from being your lover, confidante, psychologist, and closest friend into an impediment. It made perfect sense!

Or maybe, the real issue was that I was no longer useful to serve your purpose, once it was clear to you that I was not going to lend you any money to repay your debts, as you had asked me a few days before, not only because I just had enough to get by, but also because, even if I had the money, I would have not let you run away from facing the consequences of your actions.

Just when I had felt that we were starting to build something that seemed to resemble a proper relationship, you had managed to make me feel used and worthless once again.

That's the difference between pain and illusion. Pain makes you stronger. Illusion leaves you empty.

"Don't take it so hard," you told me as I stared into space with glazed eyes, numbed as I was by the contradictory messages that you had sent my way for far too long. "You are a nice person, but it is just not the right time."

"I already know that. That's not the point. There is no need to sugar-coat it to feel better about yourself," I mumbled, overwhelmed by a growing sense of void as my heart mourned a person who had never existed.

At a first look, everything you would say made perfect sense, if it wasn't for the fact that, hours or days later, you would say exactly the opposite, only to retract it all or blatantly lie every time I would catch you red-handed, to the point that I would question and blame my own judgment and perception of reality.

We had nearly reached home.

I looked at you one last time, hoping to catch a glimpse of regret or remorse in your eyes, but they were lifeless.

"Goodbye, Miad. You will never find someone who will love you as much as I did," I said, as you stopped in front of my building.

I lingered a few seconds before getting out of the car. *Don't let me go*, my heart was screaming desperately.

"I am sorry," was all you said. I had heard that line so many times that I could no longer believe it.

I took the keys out of my bag and walked towards the front door, without looking back, as you drove off and disappeared into the misty sky.

∞

"How much more do you want him to hurt you before you can let him go?" Fang asked me over dinner at our favourite Greek eatery on Headingley high street.

I didn't mention your gambling habits to her, not only because, even at such a low point in our relationship, I felt the need to protect you and avoid sharing your secrets, but also because a part of me felt deeply guilty and ashamed that not even your addictive personality was a good enough reason to get you out of my life and my heart.

Even if at first, she had given you some credit for appearing genuinely sorry for your mistakes and keen to make up for them, after I told her how enraged you had become in Brazil when you had seen me talking to other men, she lost all hope that anything good could have come out of our relationship, and she tried her best to encourage me to move on with my life.

"Don't even think he could ever change. He won't," she stated confidently, as she browsed through the mouth-watering menu.

That is what motivates many of us to carry on with our toxic relationships, as miserable as they make us feel—the hope that, with love and patience, people may become a much better version of themselves. But the truth is that change can only occur when it is initiated out of our free will, within ourselves, rather than forced upon us. And most of the time, we only feel the drive to change when we reach a turning point in our lives, like when we experience something so distressful and traumatic that it shatters our sense of self in such a profound way that we are left with no other option than to rebuild ourselves from scratch.

You, however, were in denial. Nothing I could have done and said would have made any difference because, no matter what, you would have found someone or something other than yourself to blame.

"You're right, Fang. My brain keeps telling me the same every single day. I just need to convince my heart of that," I said, sighing and pouring some Retsina wine into our glasses.

I had stayed teetotal throughout my marriage, partly out of respect for Tahir, and partly because I never felt I was missing out. But after my divorce, as my social life slowly took off, I had started drinking a glass of wine on social occasions.

"Well … for a start, you could go out, meet new people, and have a good time," she replied with her usual pragmatism.

"Yes, I'll make an effort. I'll do it for myself and for Amal. It's time to get back control of my life."

"Cheers to that!" Fang exclaimed, before clinking my glass with both hands in a celebratory gesture.

Leo

CHAPTER TWENTY-FIVE

I hadn't noticed him until he had started talking.

"Are you also Italian?" he asked, bringing me back to reality.

I gave him a puzzled look. "Yes. Are you?"

Following Fang's advice, I had signed up for a Bollywood night in an Indian street food bar near Vicar Lane, a street in the centre of Leeds dotted with Thai restaurants, supermarkets, and massage parlours. I loved Bollywood cinema, and I thought that wearing a colourful skirt and dancing through the night to exotic tunes was exactly what I needed to cheer up and forget about my complicated love life for a while.

"Yes. From the South. What about you? I'm Leo by the way. Nice to meet you."

"I'm from Rome, although I've been away for a long time."

"Right. And what brought you here?"

Every time I met a new person, I could not help but give away more information about myself than needed. I was an open book. It was like I felt that, in order to connect with someone on a deeper level, I had to gain their trust first by revealing my cards. I was telling them, *Hey. This is me. Don't be afraid. I am what you see.*

This time, however, I wasn't particularly impressed, so I preferred to cut it short.

"That's a long story," I said, before the event organiser, a bubbly Indian girl with contagious enthusiasm, encouraged us to join her on the dance floor.

"Come on guys! Let's shake those hips," she urged, pulling my hand.

I followed her keenly, feeling slightly lightheaded, as I always did after drinking a glass of wine on an empty stomach. I was a cheap date.

We danced to *Jai Ho*[25], which is often translated as "victory," a meaning I found quite promising and auspicious, given my current circumstances.

The soothing power of music, combined with the alcohol and the collective euphoria, had the effect of lifting my spirits, to the point that you did not appear in my mind, not even as a fleeting thought, throughout the night.

I was more focused on the Mediterranean-looking guy who had been staring at me cheekily from the other side of the room. I had reciprocated with a flirtatious smile before realising that he had given the same kind of attention to more than one of the girls attending the event. Still, when, before going home, he had walked up to me with a disarming grin and asked for my number, after introducing himself as a Greek thirty-something software developer who went by the name of Ioannis, I gave it to him. *A womaniser is definitely not the kind of man I need, but anything will do, as long as it helps me forget Miad.*

I kept dancing for another hour. I wanted to be so exhausted by the time I reached home that I would not have any energy left to remember my heartbreak.

I was so busy trying to have a good time that I did not even realise that Leo was still there, sneaking glances at me as I swayed my hips sensually.

∞

When, sometime later, I received a message from Leo through a social network we were both subscribed to, I didn't even remember that we had already met at the Bollywood event, nor did I remember what he looked like.

I am so sorry. My head was all over the place that night, and I am quite absent-minded anyway, I wrote, trying to apologise, although I failed to mention that, in all fairness, my head was still a complete mess.

---

[25] A Hindi song composed by Indian composer A.R. Rahman for the 2008 film *Slumdog Millionaire*.

He didn't seem to be put off by my response, which was reassuring, considering that most of the guys I had interacted with would have got offended, taking it as an unacceptable blow to their big egos.

We carried on chatting for a few days, telling each other about our respective jobs, interests, and life experiences, until, one day in early May, he invited me for a drink at a posh hotel in town.

It was Amal's birthday weekend, and Tahir had come over to attend the celebrations. After a few ups and downs, our relationship had evolved into a peaceful co-parenting partnership based on respect towards each other, the family we had built together, and the memory of what we once were as a couple.

Still, the idea that he would stay a full week at my place, coupled with the prospect of spending a Sunday afternoon handling thirty-five overexcited six-year-olds screaming and running around the party hall I had rented for the occasion, was making me restless. So when Leo suggested that we meet straight after the party, I thought that would be the perfect chance to unwind and recover from the stress of the situation.

When I got out of the taxi in front of Leeds Town Hall, where we had agreed to meet, I found him waiting for me wearing a grey shirt, black tailored trousers, and a big smile, despite the rain and the fact that I was half an hour late. I was pleasantly surprised by his confidence and laid-back attitude.

We walked together up to the hotel. He did not wear a jacket, and I did not carry an umbrella, so when we reached the main entrance, all soaked in our fancy clothes, we exchanged a complicit look, laughing at each other for our excessive optimism. Leo opened the door for me to let me in.

Nice. A real gentleman, I thought, ticking a box on the mental checklist most of us keep when we start dating.

The bar was fairly quiet, which was hardly surprising for a rainy Sunday evening at the beginning of the month. As we sat next to each other at a table at the far corner of the room, I could sense that we were both slightly embarrassed, as two people who hardly know each other are on a first date, when they find themselves in close proximity.

I let him order the wine. To me, they all tasted more or less the same anyway.

Leo went for a *Primitivo di Manduria*, a red wine from Apulia, the southern region forming the heel of Italy's boot.

"That's where my father was born!" I told him, finding the coincidence amusing.

We talked for a couple of hours in a spontaneous, friendly way. There was none of the drama that had marked my first dates with you, none of the uncontrollable attraction and chemistry that had led us to jump into bed the second time we had met, none of the violent emotions that your sheer presence would bring to surface. There were just two people getting to know each other without rushing into any conclusion too soon. It was nice for once to have a relaxed conversation with a guy over a glass of wine, without feeling that he was after something other than a chat and some good-natured banter.

Just like me, Leo loved foreign languages and literature, to the point that he had got a degree in that subject.

Coming from a small village near the hilltop city of Ragusa, in southeast Sicily, where it was hard to find a qualified job, he had decided to move abroad straight after obtaining his degree, and a long hot summer spent working as a receptionist at a local tourist resort. Thanks to his language skills, he had been offered a call centre role at the Eastern European headquarters of a global sports clothing manufacturer in Prague. Following that, he had decided to try his luck in Leeds, where he had been working in sales for the previous two years.

"Time for bed," I told Leo after realising that, if I stayed any longer, I would not have been able to wake up on time for the daily school run.

"Indeed. I also have an early start tomorrow," Leo said, winking at me.

We walked side by side to the taxi rank. Then, once I got into the cab, he saw me off, wishing me a good night.

I had a great time. We should meet again, he texted half an hour later, just as I was about to turn off my phone and get ready to sleep. I smiled, ticking another box on my list.

I had also enjoyed the night, feeling calm and at ease in his presence. The conversation had flown easily, helping distract me for a moment from the constant feeling of void that had been eating me up since our break-up. But would that have been enough to let you go once and for all? I did not think so.

Still, I wanted to give it a try.

Glad to hear that. Sure, let's do it again, I responded.

What I had found interesting about Leo was not just his determination—he had come across as a pretty focused individual—but also his independent spirit.

After a string of disastrous flings with fellow nationals in my early twenties, I had sworn to myself that I would not date an Italian man ever again in my life, put off by the *prima donna* attitude of the guys I had gone out with.

Based on my personal experience, Italian men were excessively attached to their families, particularly their mothers, from whom they rarely became truly independent until at least their late thirties, some even later, often only to replace them with another maternal figure—their girlfriends or wives.

And for an independent woman like myself, the thought of being with a *mama's boy*, who could not even look after himself, let alone a family of his own, was hardly appealing. In fact, it was a massive turn-off.

But Leo was very different from the stereotypical Italian men who populated the collective imagination, and mine. For a start, he was close to his family, but that had not prevented him from building a life of his own, away from them. He retained the traditional values that were at the core of his upbringing, but he was also aware of his place in a fast-changing world. He was loyal, genuine, and respectful. But most importantly, he was not scared of my past, nor did he feel threatened by it.

He was confident about himself enough not to fear any comparison, and without any of the arrogance and self-entitlement that characterised my previous dates. Nothing got my attention more, however, than his persistence.

I saw him again a few days after our first date. This time, he had chosen a Persian tea room just behind Leeds Kirkgate Market, one of the few places in Leeds where you could grab a bite until the early hours and chill out drinking chai from colourful glasses, or smoking shisha sitting on comfy cushions, while Middle Eastern music permeated the air through the loudspeakers.

"Perfect choice," I said with a bitter smile when, after meeting outside the town hall like the previous time, he had shared his idea.

A Persian café where everything, from the food to the tea, from the furniture to the music, reminds me of Miad is exactly what I need to try and forget him, I thought, feeling doomed.

"Why?" he asked, embarrassed, sensing the irony in my remark.

"Sorry, I was just kidding," I replied, cursing myself for never being able to bite my tongue when needed.

I wished I could have shown him the thorns that were pricking my soul. Maybe that would have helped me get rid of them. But it was too early for that. After all, we were little more than strangers, and I did not want to burden him with a weight heavier than anybody could carry. So I kept smiling, hoping that the sadness in my eyes would not give me away, even though I knew it would.

Indeed, he had gone suddenly quiet and distant, looking absorbed in his own thoughts, his mind full of questions he dared not ask, as if he was trying to figure out which one, if any, among my skeletons in the closet, he would be prepared to discover.

Despite the initial blunder, the date went well, but, by the end of the night, I knew that there was no point in going any further. *Who could I fool?*

Imagine you spend an entire day on a rollercoaster. Then they tell you it is time to get off. At first, you feel happy, because you had enough of the constant bumping and palpitations, but when you go back down, onto the ground, the world no longer looks and feels the same. How exciting it was to look at the Earth right from above!

Now everything you do seems so dull and ordinary. Nobody you meet draws any interest from you because he can never be as exciting as a rollercoaster ride. And you just feel lifeless, because all the adrenaline your body produced during the ride is no longer pumping through your veins. *How could someone who, on several occasions, had considered death as a quick-fix solution to his problems, make me feel so full of life?*

∞

I felt dizzy. My head was spinning, and my eyes were hurting. It felt like I would never arrive home. The taxi driver was going at an unbelievably low speed, stopping at every red light he could possibly catch. I could not wait to be home, to take off my clothes and the heavy make-up, slip into my heart-print fleece pyjamas, and curl up under the blankets, cuddled by the cosy and familiar warmth of my bedroom.

I had decorated it to my liking in shades of white and blue, which instilled a sense of calm and peace in my mind as soon as I crossed the doorstep. Colourful Moroccan lanterns were hanging from the ceiling, while round mosaic candleholders were displayed on the windowsill. A small rug with Arabesque designs lay at one side of the wooden king-size bed. A large butterfly painting and a hand-painted mosaic mirror finished the décor.

Will it ever stop hurting? I thought as the car finally stopped in front of my flat.

As always, it took me ages to find the keys. They would always get lost in the sea of body wipes, perfumes, business cards, lipsticks, sweets, and the other items that clutter a woman's handbag, most of which are entirely useless.

Two ramps of stairs, and there I was. Suddenly, it started raining, and I could hear the sound of leaves rustling in the wind.

I just wanted to forget and forgive, but, wherever I would go, I was haunted by your presence. Every time a cab drove by, I would take a quick glance at the driver in the front seat, hoping to meet your eyes again. Those eyes that intimidated me, teased me, and aroused me all at the same time. Those eyes I wanted so badly to erase from my memory, and yet I was holding onto the same memory with all my strength, desperately afraid that I might forget them.

I was dying to feel your arms wrapped around my body, your hands exploring every inch of my skin, to taste your kisses that had the power to awaken my most intimate emotions and bring them to life. After you were gone, I would spend hours staring at the ceiling, my entire room pervaded with your perfume. The idea that someone else could touch that body that only *I* knew so well, that body which could give me the greatest of pleasures as well as inflict the deepest pain, that body I could arouse in no time, was driving me insane.

Where are you? What have you been doing all this time, when all I wanted was to hold you in my arms again? See that cheeky smile of yours one more time? Who else could bring your senses to life without even touching you? Who else could make love to you with her mind? Who is dying to comfort your body as much as your broken soul?

CHAPTER TWENTY-SIX

One last picture and that was it. You no longer existed.

I had scanned every single drawer, wardrobe, cabinet, and shelf in my flat in search for fragments of you. I particularly loved that picture. We had taken it together during our Brazil trip on a rope swing bridge overlooking some waterfalls. We were both wearing sunglasses, but, unlike you, with a tough-guy look on your face, I was beaming.

I was wearing a sleeveless dress in a peach pink shade which brightened up my fair complexion, whereas you were bare-chested, showing off your scary tattoos and fit body. Your dark hair and beard were perfectly trimmed.

Nothing could sum up our relationship better than that picture: We were light and darkness, yin and yang, the moon and the sun, opposite yet complementary entities.

I tossed the photo into the large bin bag, along with the other traces of your presence in my house. A Japanese porcelain teacup with lid that you had given me after telling you that I liked my tea very hot. A massive black umbrella that you had insisted I take during a sudden downpour on an April afternoon, when you had dropped me off at Amal's school.

I always hated umbrellas, and on the few occasions I would take one with me, I would leave it behind in a shop or a café, only to remember about it several hours later, when I was already soaked and on my way home.

But this time was different. I had not forgotten about your umbrella, which I had safely set aside in my storage room, with the intention of giving it back to you as soon as we would meet again. Every time we met, however, I would procrastinate returning it until the following time, as if I were unconsciously looking for a pretext to see you again.

I glanced at the remaining items inside the bag: a grey sweatshirt that you had sprayed with your favourite fragrance the same rainy afternoon, so that I would always feel close to you. Even though the scent had faded away, every time I would open the wardrobe and spot your piece of clothing among mine, I could still smell it.

Some DIY tools, the decorations you had bought for Amal's aquarium, the fancy toiletries you had given me on my birthday, your toothbrush and toothpaste. The night you had told me you would leave them in my bathroom, next to mine, my eyes had lit up. To me, that tiny gesture meant much more than what it actually was. It meant *I am here to stay.*

I would return every single memory of us back to you. As childish as it sounded, I hoped that, physically separating from all the memories I was holding onto, would help me get the same cathartic feeling of closure I had experienced more than ten years before, when I had been dumped by my then-boyfriend.

I was about to tie the bag when I suddenly remembered about the goldfish, which were staring at me, looking cosy in their tank on the windowsill, unaware of my diabolical plan.

Amal would have been devastated if she came home from school to find I had given them away. *Fair enough, you are safe*, I muttered under my breath, giving them a benevolent look.

I was going to London for work later that morning, so I had a quick shower, put on my business attire, and called a taxi, asking the driver to make one stop at your home address before going to the station.

As I got back into the car, after dropping the bin bag with all your belongings on your driveway, I felt a deep sense of relief. The taxi driver hesitated a few minutes before making a U-turn and continuing the journey. "We can go now," I pressed him, not wanting to take a second glance at that house that looked too painfully familiar and had been the setting of many wild moments together.

It did not take long for you to react.

Hey. How are you? I am going to Iran for a month. Wish you all the best, you texted as I was reading the paper in the quiet coach of the 10:15 a.m. London North Eastern Railway train to London King's Cross. Anybody else would have not read anything strange or unusual into your text, but not me. I knew you too well not to understand what you were after. And I had learned over time that your *how are you* was never just that. You were not the kind of person who asked someone how they were doing just because he was genuinely interested in their well-being. There was always a reason why you would do or say something, and that reason was not the most obvious one.

This time was no exception. You were trying to play the nice guy, pretending that nothing had ever happened, in order to leave your options open. Your *how are you* was just a sneaky way to test the waters. It was a declaration of war. It meant I *want to see you, I need you, let's get back together*, and anything in-between. Just like your *sorry* was always driven by a desire to feel better about yourself and regain control over me, rather than genuine remorse for the hurt your actions would cause. But this was an old trick for me. A trick that may have worked with the old Sofia, not the one that you had contributed to shaping by bringing out my vulnerabilities and exploiting them to your advantage.

True, I was not ready to let you go, but I was not ready to see you either, to feel wanted and rejected at the same time once again. I deleted the text and carried on reading.

∞

I did not hear from you, neither did I see Leo, for the rest of the summer. To tell the truth, he had texted me every single day since our last date, until one day, sensing that I had no intention to knock down the walls I had built around myself, he stopped.

That was when I remembered the words of someone I had dated for a month, shortly after our first proper break-up.

You push away everybody that genuinely cares about you. If you keep behaving like this, you will be alone for the rest of your life, the guy had told me on our fourth date, after I had realised that, as much as I tried, I could not get you out of my mind.

At first, I had not paid much attention to his words, since I was convinced that he had uttered them out of spite, triggered by his hurt ego. However, as the days went by, those words were still reverberating in my heart. Not because I was scared of turning into a lonely old spinster.

I was so used to living in my inner world, and doing whatever I wanted, that solitude was not a particularly daunting prospect.

It was because that had not been the first time someone had told me that, and it got me thinking. Maybe, after all, me and you were not so different.

What did I keep running away from?

I was adamant to find out. It was time to rediscover myself and try to make sense of the previous couple of years.

Amal was spending the holidays in Dubai with Tahir, and although I was tempted to join them, I booked myself a one-week solo stay in Malta, hoping that the Mediterranean sea salt that is still being harvested on its shores would help heal my wounds faster.

I loved solo travelling. Being able to explore, sightsee, eat, sunbathe, party, and do whatever you felt like at your own pace, and without having to take anything into account other than your own needs was very liberating. Soon, however, I would discover that this freedom, which in the Western world we sometimes take for granted and other times overrate, is just an illusion if it does not start from within. We can travel to the end of the world, but if we do not empty our baggage of all the fears and worries that had prompted us to set on our journey in the first place, our spirit will never truly be free.

I spent my days trying to numb those fears with new faces, casual dates, nights out, anything that would temporarily inebriate me with the euphoria of the unknown. But if they ask you to imagine a lemon and then suddenly tell you to stop thinking about it, would you stop? Or would you see lemons all around you?

You were my lemon.

∞

The days had already become shorter and the nights colder, and the stores were swamped with compulsive shoppers in autopilot mode, driven by the collective frenzy that takes hold of people in the run-up to Christmas, when I met Leo again at a Halloween party in a private club, organised by the Leeds expat community.

I had spotted him in the crowd shortly after I had arrived, but I pretended not to know him. I was still feeling guilty for having put him in a position to end things between us well before they had even started.

I carried on drinking wine with my Spanish friend as we discussed our favourite work by Pedro Almodóvar. "I really loved *Women on the Verge of a Nervous Breakdown*. You must watch it!" Carmen, a lecturer from Valencia who taught Media Studies at Leeds University said, when I told her I had not had a chance to see it. I was a big fan of Almodóvar. His passion, irreverent humour, unconventional surrealism, conflicted characters, disdain for social and religious norms—all resonated deeply with my own life experiences.

"Well … I can certainly relate to the theme right now," I joked, before adding: "My favourite is *Volver*. Such a brilliant performance by Penélope Cruz!"

"*Ciao*, how are you doing?" Leo chimed in, looking visibly happy to see me again.

I looked at him as Carmen suddenly retreated, assuming it was one of those moments when three is a crowd.

Unlike him, on the other hand, I was embarrassed and struggling to maintain eye contact.

"Hey … it's been a while. I am good. What about you?" I said, trying not to sound excessively friendly, fearing that he could interpret that as an encouraging hint.

"Sorry if I disappeared like that," he said. "I shouldn't have done that, but I had a tough period. I was about to give it all up and move back home."

I was speechless. This guy was standing in front of me, worried that my distant attitude was due to the fact that, after a few dates where he had behaved impeccably—like the true gentleman he was—and after texting me every single day for weeks and being given the cold shoulder repeatedly, he had understandably given up and vanished into the ether.

"No worries. It's okay. I should apologise actually. I was not in a good place either," I said, trying to convince myself that now I had moved to a better place.

His words had struck a chord with me. It was the first time since we had met that he had shown me a vulnerable side. Until that point, he had come across as someone with a high level of self-control, who seemed immune to the emotional ups and downs and moments of self-doubt which make us so extraordinarily human.

"No, really," Leo insisted. "It was not a nice thing to do. Do you fancy going for a drink sometime so I can make it up to you?"

Oh gosh! That was not what I expected he would say.

I thought that he would suggest we stay friends, or on the contrary, that he would end up hating me for being such a stuck-up snob. Not that he would invite me to go out again.

"Sorry to be blunt," I replied. "But I'm not sure what you are after exactly."

"What do you mean? I just want us to get to know each other," he said.

"I see, but we already got to know each other."

"Fair enough. Then let's get to know each other *again*."

"What for?" I asked, trying to push him to his limits so that he would eventually desist. "We have gone out a few times and there was no spark between us. What makes you think that this time would be different? I know what I want at this point in my life and don't want to waste my time."

I knew that my harsh words would have hurt him, like I also knew that he had done nothing wrong to deserve them. He was not responsible for the sense of frustration and humiliation, the overall distrust of the male species, and the insecurities that someone before him had instilled in me. And if I really knew what I wanted, why was I always rowing in the opposite direction to *that*?

"Maybe you are right. Let's leave it," Leo said, his light brown eyes filled with disappointment.

A part of me hoped that he would tell me I was wrong, that he would show me he was different from all the others, so when he turned his back and walked away, I felt defeated, considering that as further proof that whoever entered my life would walk out on me sooner or later.

CHAPTER TWENTY-SEVEN

You came back, just when I had started giving up on you.

"Block him," my sister suggested when I told her you were still bothering me.

No, I couldn't. Blocking you meant escaping from myself and my fears, whereas I wanted to prove to myself that I was much stronger than that. That you no longer had control over my thoughts and my life.

I would wait for as long as it took for you to stop pushing my boundaries and leave me alone forever. And even if you never let go of something you felt entitled to, every time you would get in touch, your grip would loosen, until one day I would wake up from my bad dream and see you for what you were, rather than the idealised projection that, day after day, you had planted in my mind.

No, I would not run away even if it drove me insane.

Moments after the first text arrived, I was pervaded with an overwhelming feeling of impending doom, such was the powerful strength of the emotions you could provoke in me. I could feel you from miles away.

I wanted to call you since the protests in Hong Kong started, but I tried not to bother you. Are you okay?

I had mentioned to you about my upcoming work trip to Hong Kong last time we had met.

You did the right thing, I texted back.

Once you had realised that I was not willing to go back to you, at least not on your terms, you gave me the silent treatment, seeing my defiance as an unacceptable blow to your ego, only to reappear a few weeks later, hoping that I had changed my mind.

But how could I change my mind if you had not given me any of the answers I was looking for?

That was when you decided to change strategy. You did your best to convince me that you had changed, that you were a different man.

I saw your text as soon as I opened my eyes on a freezing morning in late January, one of those mornings when a lie-in cocooned in the cosy warmth of your blankets is a temptation too strong to resist.

I missed you so, so much, the text read.

My heart thumped, but I did not want to respond on an impulse. Instead, I took some time to reflect on what to say.

Before meeting you, I used to have neither filters nor barriers. I would say whatever crossed my mind. But after seeing how cunning and calculating you could be, how you would twist every word I would say and use it against me, I had become much more self-conscious in my interactions with you. They were not just regular conversations. They were emotionally draining mind games.

But there was a question that had been swirling around my head every single day since our break-up. I put the kettle on and fed the goldfish, as I did every morning before waking up Amal for school. Then I replied: *If you missed me, why did you let me go?*

I think we should see each other and talk.

Why? What for? Nothing would ever change. We just keep driving each other crazy. I think it is better we stay away, I said, fighting with all my strength not to let you catch me off guard.

Can I call you?

No, you can't. I am having breakfast and you are going to make me late for the school run, was my response. But just as I was about to press the send button, the phone started ringing. You were at it again, crossing my boundaries, as you got in and out of my life at your own leisure.

I stared at the phone for a few seconds, until, eventually, I picked up.

"Sorry, but I just wanted to hear your voice. You don't seem very happy to hear from me, though," you said, after noticing that its tone was icy.

"What do you expect, Miad? Do you realise how much you hurt me? Shall I refresh your memory? I am not your toy. You can't take me and throw me whenever you feel like." I fought hard to contain the anger that had been growing inside of me since I had last seen you.

"I am sorry if I hurt you. I did not mean to. I was not very emotionally stable at that point. But now it is different. Lots of things changed. I have been working as a taxi driver on top of the mechanic job and I am paying off my debts, you know? I want to try and work things out between us."

"Really? And if you did not mean to hurt me, why did you keep doing it over and over again? How could I trust you again?"

I no longer cared about keeping my cool.

"You know, I even missed fighting with you," you said, laughing. "How bad must I have been for you not to believe my words? I guess time will show you that you can trust me."

"Maybe it's too late for that."

"What do you mean?"

"I mean that I am seeing someone at the moment," I replied, wondering why I always felt the need to give you explanations you did not even deserve.

That was true. After my tactless remarks at the Halloween party, I had met Leo again a couple of months later at a New Year's event, and despite the initial embarrassment, we had laughed at the irony of the situation, wondering why, in a city of over eight hundred thousand residents, we kept bumping into each other when, statistically speaking, it would have been much more probable (and advisable) not to see each other again.

"We are doomed," Leo had joked, as we sat on a sofa in a quiet corner of the bar where the event was taking place.

His friendly and laid-back manners made me feel good, and safe. By the end of the night, as he accompanied me to the taxi that was waiting for me outside the bar and wished me good night, I realised I had not laughed so much in a very long time, busy as I was crying over a ghost that had turned me into his shadow.

Was it right to close the door to him, just because, at that point, I was not ready to start a new relationship?

For the time being, all I wanted was his friendship, not the kind of hybrid post-modern opportunistic exchange which was now standard practice between two people who wanted all the benefits of a relationship without any of the commitment and responsibilities.

Just the genuine, unadulterated bond which unites two people with similar interests and matching characters, and that can, over time, grow into a feeling of love. And if he was happy to give his friendship to me, why did I have to give it up?

"Aw right," you said nonchalantly. You would have never admitted to me or to yourself that the idea I could be with someone else was a major hit to your ego, but I knew that deep down, you were fuming. "You are not in love with him anyway." Same defiant arrogance. "There are many things missing in him. I feel that," you added, as you tried to convince me that I could have not loved anybody else other than you.

How presumptuous was that?!

"It is too early to say whether I love him or not. I am not like you. I can't stop feeling for someone from one day to another, but that does not mean I cannot try and move on with my life."

"Well … if you think about someone else, you should be with the person you think about," you pointed out, as if that was the only logical conclusion.

"Pity that that person does not want to be with me," I noted, shocked that you could distort the facts to such extent that I, rather than you, was to blame for no longer being together.

"Who said that? You never know what happens in the future. We cannot move in together from one day to another, especially after all this time apart. But we can start seeing each other again and see how it goes."

"Did I ever ask you to live together? Did I ask you to marry me? No, that has never been the point. You always knew that since my divorce, I stopped making long-term plans because life never quite goes to plan. All I wanted was for us to be there for each other and to feel that you wanted that as much as I did. I wanted to live fully in our present, together, to feel you close to me rather than always keep me at a distance—"

"I just felt under pressure," you said, interrupting me.

It was one of the few times since our first meeting that we had been able to have what seemed an open, heart-to-heart conversation, and even though I did not really believe you could ever change, your words had insinuated some doubt into that irrational part of my mind that could not let you go. It took another few weeks of back-and-forth, though, before I finally agreed to meet again.

After all, the time we had been together had been a hard-core survival course. We had seen the worst of each other, the dark and the sunny side. What other evil was inside of you that I had not already been prepared to unveil and deal with?

Amal was at school, and I was struggling to concentrate on my work, as I had had a rough night thinking about our long-due reunion.

As was always the case with you, I was thrilled and edgy in equal measure. It was only ten o'clock, and we were due to meet at my place two hours later. I had rehearsed every detail in my head so many times.

I scrubbed every inch of my skin, mixing olive oil and salt in equal parts, just like an ancient Greek lady would have done to keep her skin soft and clean. I wanted my body to be as smooth as our relationship had never been. I generously sprayed myself with an exotic fragrance which evoked oriental mysteries. I applied a coconut mask onto my hair. I loved the sweet scent of coconut. It reminded me of summer escapades.

As a child, every summer my parents would take me holidaying along Salento's sandy beaches, where seasonal peddlers slalomed between rows of beachgoers screaming *Cocco bello!*—pretty coconut— to attract their attention and encourage them to savour its sweet flesh. As I took a bite of the exotic fruit, I would feel transported to an unfamiliar world made of unusual yet enticing flavours, which would not only stimulate my senses but also arouse my innate curiosity. It was the same curiosity that, years later, would propel me to experiment with food and discover new cuisines and new tastes, taking the phrase *variety is the spice of life* and bringing it to new heights.

I wore a burgundy satin wrap dress, which matched my nail polish and lipstick, paired with sheer black tights and suede ankle strap court shoes.

As you used to do every time we would meet, you texted me to let me know you were five minutes away from my place.

I was counting down the seconds with a knot in my stomach, a thumping heart, and a dizzy head, which had already started regretting my decision. The intercom rang as I was putting on my favourite pair of gold-plated chandelier-drop earrings with red crystal beads. I took one final look at myself in the mirror and felt pleased with the image it reflected.

It was showdown time.

As I opened the door and found you in front of me, looking sexy in your denim shirt and beige slim-fit cotton trousers, and drenched in Chanel *Allure*, you gave me your warmest smile and immediately wrapped me in a tight embrace, which left me breathless, kissing me gently on my lips before I could even say hi. We stayed like that, our bodies firmly glued to each other, for what felt like an eternity.

There was all of us in that simple gesture: There was pain, despair, passion, forgiveness. There were all the words we had left unsaid and all those we should have never uttered. There were dramatic goodbyes that never tasted like farewells because the trail of sadness and destruction they left behind would drag on for months, making it impossible to achieve any sense of closure. There was just me and you, leaving the world outside and allowing ourselves to be just that for an hour or two.

"I am so happy to see you," you said, as you lifted me off the ground and carried me to the sofa in the lounge. "Since you did not want to see me, every time I was thinking about you, I would close my eyes and imagine you … I could *feel* you."

Your eyes, which the day we had broken up looked still and lifeless, had regained their sparkle. I stared at them, hoping I could read the answers that your mouth would not give me. I did not want to give you any further certainties than those you already had by admitting that I had done the same, imagining you every night as I lay in bed, often until I cried myself to sleep. That would have once again put me in a weaker position. And I could not let down my defences. Not too soon.

"I missed everything about you … the way you touched me … the way you are … so passionate, so romantic," you said.

"That's because I *felt* so strongly about you," I replied, deliberately using the past tense to get the message across.

I knew that by praising me for my qualities, you were comparing me to the other girls you had been with during our time apart, who, judging from your words, supposedly lacked such qualities. I was certainly not over the moon about the fact that the man I loved had come back to me because he had felt he could have not found anything better, but on the other hand, I did not feel entitled to say anything, considering that I had also tried to fill the void that your absence had created with other people. Unlike you, though, I was doing that because you had left me with no other option than forgetting about you, not because that was what I really wanted.

"Come closer to me," you said, pulling me towards you, since, just like the second time we had met, I was sitting in the far corner of my sofa.

As you held me firmly in your arms, I could feel your heart racing. "I stayed up until three in the morning," you said.

"Why? Was it down to the thrill of seeing me again?"

"Yes. I was nervous," you answered with a serious look.

We cuddled each other without saying a word for a good ten minutes. We were not good at verbal communication anyway. We were not made to be friends, to make small talk, to wish each other Happy Birthday or Merry Christmas. But when we let our body language do the talking, it was magical.

How could such an unpredictable and emotionally unstable individual have the power to calm me down with just a hug? There was something inexplicably familiar about you, the smell of your skin, the sensations that the contact with your body would generate, but I still couldn't pinpoint what that was.

The touches, which at first were tender and gentle, suddenly became more sensual and unrestrained, until passion and desire took over, and we made love like there was no tomorrow, with all the desperate longing of two lovers who have been apart for too long and know that they may never meet again.

Once we had given free rein to our most visceral impulses, you hugged me and slowly rested my head on your chest. I, in turn, wrapped my legs around you and grabbed your hand, squeezing it into mine, as if I wanted to make sure I was not dreaming. I wasn't indeed. It was all real, right in front of my eyes.

CHAPTER TWENTY-EIGHT

The sinking feeling started as soon as I picked up the phone, even though, at first, I tried to push it away.

"Hey … are you okay?" I said, noticing some unease in your voice.

"Yes, just had a busy day at work. I am sorry, but I can't do this."

Less than twenty-four hours had passed since our reunion, and you had already gone cold and distant again. My recurring nightmare had turned into reality.

I tried to formulate a question, but the words got stuck in my throat.

"It's been fun, but I want to move on with my life," you said, pronouncing each word with petrifying indifference.

A train hit me at full speed. *Was this the same person who just a few hours before was equally ecstatic and excited at the thought of seeing me again?*

"Are you crazy or what?" I screamed. "You have been chasing me for weeks, going on about how much you had missed me, and, when I finally decided to give you one last chance, you tell me it's over? I can't believe you really did this to me. Not again."

"You see? It is *your* fault. You always take things too hard."

Here we go again, I thought, blaming me for something you had done.

"Does it make you happy? I really want to know. How does it feel to use people who care about you for your own selfish needs? If all you wanted was a shag, I am sure you had plenty of other options. You did not need *me* for that. There was no need to reopen a wound that had just started turning into a scar."

"Oh please, grow up! I have never used you. I left many girls in my life, but none of them reacted like you."

This time it was you that was doing all the shouting, furious at me for having dared to call your bluff. "Hope you don't slag me off with your friends now," you said.

I was gutted. Even at such a critical moment, all you cared about was your public image.

"You are the most toxic person I have ever met in my life. I wish I had never met you," I said, even though I did not really mean it. That would have meant going against my own beliefs, that there was always a reason why something happens to us, a hidden lesson to be learned, that could turn even the most traumatic experiences into once-in-a-lifetime chances.

"Look, I would have come and told you this in person, but I am really tired, and I have a headache. Goodbye." And you hung up.

We cannot expect someone else to take care of our past traumas and vulnerabilities, to satisfy our own physical or emotional needs, to be responsible for our own love choices. What we can hope is that that person will avoid pulling those wounds apart and pouring salt into them time and again.

Pain, however, was the only feeling you could give others. Instead of killing them with one shot though, you would take a dagger and stab them a thousand times, cutting fresh wounds all over their body, so deep they reached their core. It hurt, it hurt like crazy, but over time, these wounds would slowly heal, and your prey would start feeling their old selves again. That's when you would come back and repeat the whole process.

Finally, when you made sure they felt as empty and desperate as you, once all their positive energy had been drained, you would leave, only to return a few days later to offer the illusion that only *you* could heal the wounds *you* had caused in the first place.

"I don't want to hurt you," you would tell me every time you realised you had pushed me to the very limit, to the point that it was impossible to go any further.

But how could I not feel broken?

It was all clear. It was all part of an evil plan aimed at taking revenge and punishing me for having hurt your fragile ego with my rejections. You wanted to prove to yourself and to me that you still had the upper hand in our relationship. You wanted to have the final say. To be able to end things and start them again at your convenience, because that was the only way for you to feel good about yourself, to feed off people's emotions in order to get your narcissistic supply.

But even though, by then, I had lost every single hope that you could ever feel any true remorse for your behaviour that would lead to change, accepting that the person you had loved with all of yourself—believing that you could see good inside of him that nobody else could—had used you, manipulated you, and finally discarded you like an old cloth when he no longer needed you, was a burden too heavy to carry.

You had stolen my essence, including and especially, my zest for life.

What had happened to that feisty girl who used to be the life of the party? Who would burst into laughter at anything silly she had herself done? Who had toughened up so much that nothing except death scared her anymore? The girl who her English Literature teacher had once described as *someone who never gives up?*

That girl was now just a lifeless shadow of her own self. She had lost her sparkle like a magic wand that has lost its magic, and was now completely useless. You had managed to take out on me all the anger and resentment that you harboured, as if I were just a dump where people throw anything they don't want anymore. And that anger, which this time was directed towards myself rather than you for letting it happen, was consuming me day after day. It was eating me up like a cancer, making my cheeks, once chubby and rosy, look hollow and pale.

The bullet you fired had made a big hole inside my soul, and the more I tried to mend it and fill it with nice things and nice people, the bigger it would get. I had wanted you so desperately that I had ended up losing myself to find you.

But then I would think about Amal and my whole family. I could not let them down. I loved them too much.

As for me, did I love myself? Before meeting you, I thought I did. But now, I was no longer sure. You had eroded my self-esteem to such extent that I could no longer trust my own instincts to discern right from wrong. I lost faith in everything and everybody. I swore to myself that I would never let someone close to my heart again. I erected walls so thick around me that not even my friends could get through.

Except one.

Throughout my turmoil, Leo was there, by my side, day after day, carefully tiptoeing into my life and taking me under his reassuring wing as if I were an injured bird that could no longer fly, looking after me with unwavering patience and devotion and making me feel loved and accepted like I had never felt before. And the more I was trying to push him away from me, to build barriers between us in an attempt to discourage him from pursuing our relationship, the more he would chase me with greater determination, as if to say: *I am here and I am not going to let you go.*

I was finding his resolve unnerving.

How could he be so unflappable at all times? Why did he not feel threatened by my past like everybody else? Why did he not run away?

I struggled to answer those questions. I was angry at him for not being the kind of man I had so far been attracted to, a man whose words and acts were dictated by his impulses, pride, and ego, which often were just shining armour disguising deep feelings of insecurity.

But Leo was different. He did not *need* all of that. He was not afraid of being himself, of showing me his limits and imperfections. He was not going to change *for* me, but at the same time, he was willing to take a step *towards* me whenever needed.

And as time went by, his discreet yet constant presence in my life knocked down each of my defensive walls, and I started to feel my old self again.

I tried to make up for all the time I had wasted dwelling on the past by giving free rein to my creativity. I took flamenco lessons to unleash the fire that had been destroying me day after day. I worked on some business projects that had been lying in my drawer a long time. I started writing in an attempt to distance myself from my thoughts and get rid of them. I did anything I possibly could to keep my brain occupied.

Did I manage to forget you? No, I did not. I kept thinking about you every waking moment. When I was not thinking about you, you would appear in my dreams, leaving me in a state of despair when, after waking up suddenly in the middle of the night, I would realise it had only been a product of my imagination, as my arms reached out for yours in my bed, but could not find you.

Some nights I felt more alert than others. On those nights, I felt your presence stronger than ever. I could not help but feel ashamed and guilty for my own thoughts and tried to fight as hard as I could to let you go once and for all, but the more I tried to push the thought of you out of my head, the more it would come back stronger and more vivid, defying me with the careless arrogance that was rooted so deeply in your personality.

How could I still be thinking about you after all this time, especially when someone was giving me all the love, care, and protection I had always wanted from you? I felt that I was betraying him and myself.

Leo was everything I had always looked for. A man who would make me feel valued as much as desired. Someone who would not be afraid of expressing his feelings. Who would not walk away if we had an argument but would rather try to bridge our differences. Someone patient and kind, who could put up with my mood swings. Who could cheer me up on a bad day. Who would be loyal and brave.

What was holding me back?

∞

I GET KNOCKED DOWN BUT I GET UP AGAIN, read the neon lighting on the side wall of the revamped Leeds Playhouse building.

We drove past the modern apartment blocks near the BBC Yorkshire Broadcasting Centre, and into town, as we headed to the Trinity shopping district on a busy Saturday morning for a little retail therapy. It was nearly Christmas again. Another year had gone by.

"Can I get a treat from the arts and crafts shop? I want to make an advent calendar for my teddies … Please mummy, please!" Amal exclaimed from the back seat with a pleading look, fluttering her eyelashes for good measure.

I turned back and gave her a frown of disapproval to which she responded with an irresistible angelical smile. She knew how to get her way.

"Fair enough. Just a small one," I said.

Leo reached out for my hand and smiled at me tenderly, as I admitted defeat.

I looked out the window and observed the stream of strangers who were going about their daily business. At first glance, they all looked the same: ordinary people who were just getting on with life. But if one looked closer, they could notice that their faces revealed different stories. Some looked sad, as if they were fighting a battle whose wounds were not to be found on the skin; others looked happy, displaying the carefree excitement typical of the young and the inexperienced.

There were forty-somethings whose faces had been prematurely aged by a life of excesses and regrets.

Teenagers who strived to hide their insecurities behind layers of fashionable clothes and expensive trainers, which provided them with a reassuring illusion of belonging against the uncertainties of their developing identity.

There were couples walking hand in hand, pausing from time to time to make goo-goo eyes at each other, and others whose rolling eyes and furrowed eyebrows gave away the tension between them, as time and disagreements weakened the strength of the fondness they once had for each other.

If one had talked to them, some may have come across as friendly and kind, others would have sounded nasty and arrogant. But all of them would have been unique in their distinct individuality while their woes, joys, and experiences would have seemed so unbelievably familiar—such is the sweeping universality of the human condition.

Maybe that is the point, I thought as we reached our destination.

Each of us had been made a victim and an oppressor by our unique circumstances, but deep down, we were the same: vulnerable human beings who, like the children we once were, just wanted to be loved, accepted, and forgiven.

And as hard as it was, forgiving you and forgiving myself was the only way forward.

CHAPTER TWENTY-NINE

*H*ow *are you?* A WhatsApp message popped up on my screen as soon as I switched on my phone.

It took me a few seconds to realise who the sender was.

Unlike the past, this time I did not feel any thump in my heart or butterflies in my stomach, just sheer panic.

On an impulse, I clicked on the profile picture. It showed a man in his late thirties wearing a black T-shirt and a pair of jeans, his heavily tattooed arms leaning on the edge of a bathroom basin. He was staring at the image of himself reflected in the mirror with a complacent grin on his face.

I shook my head and sighed bitterly. That picture was worth a thousand words.

I had archived our conversations a year before, so that I would not have to read your name or see your face every time I opened the app, but I was not yet ready to delete them because they were the only tangible proof of your existence. And I was afraid that, if I deleted them, my memories would have faded away too.

And if we forget about the past, how can we learn from it?

∞

As you talked, I was staring at my perfectly manicured maroon nails. I could not even bring myself to look you in the face.

Why was I there anyway? Why did I feel the need to go back to that house, where we had lived so many wild and carefree moments, and that had also been the stage of our fiercest fights? Maybe I needed to make sure that it all had been real, rather than a product of my mind, playing cruel tricks on me.

I needed some closure, but would it have ever been?

It was as if going back there, I was trying to go back in time and take back that part of me that you had stolen years before, even though, deep down, I knew that my efforts would have been in vain. You were too greedy and selfish to give it back to me.

Nearly everything in that place had changed, just like your ever-changing personality. You had fitted a new dark walnut kitchen, bought a bigger plasma TV, got rid of the paper shade floor lamp that had been standing next to the sofa, and rearranged the rest of the furniture. But even if the environment had changed, everything else, including yourself, was just as I remembered it.

If you cannot change something, change yourself is what virtually all psychology books tell you. And this is exactly what had happened.

You welcomed me in a short white bathrobe.

"Sorry, but I was just having a bath," you said, even though, knowing you and judging from your perfectly dry hair and body, I would have not been surprised that you had staged that scene just to show how good you looked in your revealing garment.

But that did not make any difference. I was not there to massage your ego.

I wanted to see you to face my demons and sever the umbilical cord that kept pulling me back towards you, firmly anchored to the past, preventing me from making the most of the new life that I had started with a new person.

However, the moment I sat there, on your sofa, as you offered me a glass of orange juice and got yourself a beer, I regretted being there in the first place, feeling extremely uncomfortable and out of place. I closed my eyes for a couple of seconds. I saw Leo, Amal, and the family we were building together—the one I had always dreamt of—and I felt like running to them as fast as I could.

"My mum left her scarf here last night, and I forgot to give it back to her," you said, pointing at the colourful piece of fabric hidden somewhere behind the sofa, that I would have never even noticed if you had not acknowledged its existence.

In another life, I would have found your apparently random remark odd, and would have unconsciously wondered why you felt the need to share that irrelevant detail with me as soon as I had set foot in your house, but now that your mask had slipped off, everything was making perfect sense.

Yours was just a subtle yet deliberate attempt at instilling doubts in my mind. You wanted to lead me to think that there were other girls out there that were casually leaving behind their *scarves* at your place at night, just like I had left my *earrings* at yours on many occasions.

It was your way to tell me that you were sought after on the dating market, and that I should have felt honoured that you were still giving me your time and attention.

Leo, my inner voice started whispering as your empty words filled the air.

How could someone be so insecure that the only way he can feel good about himself is to bring a fellow human being down? I wondered, as you kept going on about a certain female friend of yours that you had called earlier that day to see how she was. I was not sure if you had forgotten having mentioned to me that the girl in question was someone you used to sleep with, or if, once again, you had deliberately dropped her name in the conversation to trigger a jealous reaction.

Leo, the voice grew louder.

Since your allusions had not resulted in the response you had hoped for, you picked up the phone and started chatting to your workmate, babbling on about some favour you had done for him and laughing loudly.

I know this strategy very well too, I thought.

You would use it every time you felt offended because I had supposedly stepped out of line. You would deliberately ignore me like a kid who covers his ears when they don't want to hear something that irritates them.

I got up while you were still on the phone. I had seen it all.

"What are you doing?" you asked me, as you abruptly ended the conversation with your friend, like you had done with me many times, and followed me to the main door.

I gave you one final look. Your eyes were hollow and inexpressive, and I could not find any trace of the sparkle that had once made me fall in love with them.

"I am leaving," I replied matter-of-factly.

You stared at me with a glazed, imperturbable look. "I hope you will forgive me," you said.

Tears started rolling down my cheeks as I hugged you one last time. This time it was a farewell.

I was mourning the illusion that had fuelled all my hopes and dreams for days, months, and years. The death of a charming prince who, beneath the shining armour, had always remained an ugly frog, despite all my kisses. The fantasy that had been filling every waking moment of my life with a rollercoaster of emotions and now, as the cold, bitter truth sank in, had left me empty and drained.

In the space of a moment, as I walked out the door and got into the taxi that was waiting for me, I realised why I had always felt so deeply connected to you, as if you were part of my own family. It was because, every time you walked out on me in such an abrupt and insensitive manner, I would relive all the feelings of frustration and abandonment that I had experienced when, as a little child, my parents would fight for hours on end over the pettiest things, making me feel anxious and powerless as I watched them yelling angrily at each other.

As I grew up, my rebellious spirit directed the same anger and resentment that they had showed to each other, towards them. It was the irrational fear of losing control, of feeling vulnerable and defenceless, at the mercy of your explosive outbursts that had prevented me from letting you go.

I had figured out that, if I managed to fix our relationship, I would have finally been able to fix that part of me that was still haunted by those childhood memories.

The pain that you had gone through, and were now inflicting on others, resonated so deeply with me because that pain was also mine. And if I let it go, a piece of me would have gone with it. And I was not ready for that to happen.

But that night, I saw it clearly. I had to stop fighting myself and accept my feelings rather than try to push them away. I had to forgive you and forgive myself. I did not need to forget about you to be happy. I could have not done that anyway. You were a part of me like it was my arm or my leg.

And can you cut a part of your body just because it hurts? No, you were there to stay, like all the good and bad things I had experienced in my life. You would always occupy a place very deep inside my heart but that was okay. My heart was big enough to make room for new emotions. They would have been different from the ones I had lived with you but still worth living.

When we were together, we were just bringing out the worst in each other. But at least now that we were apart, I could cherish the good memories of our time together, holding onto a few sweet images that were stuck in my head and would probably stay there forever, without experiencing all the negative emotions that your intoxicating presence would trigger.

"Are you okay? You look sad," the taxi driver said as soon as I stepped into the car.

"I've had better days," I replied.

"What's the matter, dear? You can tell me about it. I have seen it all during my ten years as a taxi driver," he said.

I smiled and thanked him for his concern.

That's the beauty of life, I thought. When something bad makes you lose hope in humanity, you will always come across some random act of kindness that will restore your faith once again, to remind you that good and evil are both part of the trade-off we need to make, in order to enjoy and appreciate this wonderful ride.

The taxi turned onto the main road, and your house disappeared into the darkness.

I took the phone out of my bag, deleted any trace of our conversations, and blocked your number.

I no longer needed it. I had already found my answers.

∞

The next day, as I soon as I woke up, I turned on the stereo and started dancing to the rhythm of *Bailando*[26] like there was no tomorrow, shaking my hips vigorously as my hair swayed in the air. I carried on until I was sweaty and out of breath, overwhelmed with a feeling of happiness and contentment.

I had won. You were no longer able to take hold of my thoughts and emotions, and inhabit them, like a squatter occupies a home that does not belong to him. I had broken free, and the awareness that you were no longer in control of my mind was enough to make me want to scream with joy.

I knew I was stronger than all the pain you had inflicted on me to try and break me from day one. And you knew that too.

That's why you had tried to take everything you could from me: my body, my zest for life, my soul, even my newly found love. To isolate me and make me feel desperate enough to crave your presence and scream your name during my darkest hours.

But that was all behind. I had broken all the chains that had enslaved me for far too long and was now ready to run wild and free once again.

---

[26] Song by Spanish singer and songwriter Enrique Iglesias, released on the album *Sex and Love* (2014).

CHAPTER THIRTY

It was a cold yet bright morning in early October. The gusts of wind were stroking my cheeks, making them blush, and as I walked fast through the communal park opposite my flat, I could hear the sound of leaves rustling behind me.

As usual, we were late for school.

Even though I would set the alarm at 7:15 every morning, I would end up getting up half an hour later and spending the following half an hour trying to make up for the lost time. I admired the other mums who, at that time of the day, were able to engage in deep conversations outside the school building, wearing big smiles on their faces, their hair looking stylish and shiny.

I could barely drag myself out from under my soft geometric-patterned duvet, throw on the first set of clothes I would find in my wardrobe, wash my face, and hide my puffy eyes and untamed hair behind a pair of dark sunglasses and a black woolly hat. No, I was definitely not a morning person.

In fact, before 9 a.m., my social skills could not stretch beyond a grumbled *G'morning*, which on good days would be accompanied by a hint of a smile. Even as a child, I would dread the moment my mum would wake me up to get ready for school, switching on the lights before repeating several times: "*Amore*, it is time to get up."

I was literally counting down the days to the end of my school years.

Not only because I never particularly enjoyed school, but also because I was looking forward to the day when I would not have to wake up at

6:30 a.m. ever again. Ironically, nearly thirty years later, I would find myself giving the same *hurry up, it's late!* talk to my own daughter.

When we arrived in front of the school gate, we rang the bell but, as happened virtually every time we were running late, the gate did not open.

Someone up there must derive sadistic pleasure from watching people enduring all sorts of mishaps when they go about their daily lives, I thought.

As Murphy's Law brilliantly puts it, *whatever can go wrong, will go wrong.*

We waited for a good five minutes, but nobody answered.

I looked through the gate, hoping to spot some human figure across the top playground, but there was no one in sight.

Just then, as confused thoughts of the hundreds of things I was supposed to do that day were crowding my mind, I had my eureka moment.

If you can't beat them, join them, I thought. After all, one could not waste their lives waiting for a gate to open. And if it did not open, did it really matter?

No, it made no sense chasing something that I may or may not have achieved, frantically running towards an indefinite point in the future. Life was not a race. The destination did not matter in the slightest.

What mattered, though, was the journey.

I was standing there, in front of a closed gate, taking in the beautiful scenery around me. The yellow and purple leaves falling from the trees, the clear blue sky, the busy road pulsating with life. I closed my eyes for a second or two and just enjoyed that perfect moment, pervaded with a feeling of calm and peacefulness.

When I opened my eyes again, I saw Amal smiling at me. I smiled back.

Suddenly, I did not care that she was running late for school, and I was running late for my daily commitments. I did not care about the past and I did not care about the future. All I cared for was that instant.

I caught a glimpse of the image reflected on the window of a car parked in front of the school gate. All I could see was a woman content with life, who had finally accepted her past and made peace with it, no longer beating herself up, overwhelmed with remorse and guilt.

∞

Leo carefully listened to me recounting my busy day as he finely chopped the onions, tomatoes, and coriander, and squeezed the lime into the mortar where he had placed the mashed avocados. His guacamole had no equal.

"Eventually," I told him, "Amal's history teacher appeared from nowhere and let us in. But funnily enough, when I went back home, the same happened with our flat door. I was about to force the door open, when I looked at the number and realised I was on the floor above ours." I laughed, embarrassed, as I lined up the enchiladas in a baking dish and put them in the oven.

"What a day! You are hopeless!" Leo teased me, before wrapping me tightly in his arms.

It was Friday evening, my favourite time of the week. I loved the mix of calm and anticipation that followed the frenzy of hectic working days. After all, *to await a pleasure, is itself a pleasure*[27].

"Can we play Monopoly until dinner is ready?" Amal asked as she ran into the kitchen.

"Yes, let's go and see who is going to beat mummy," Leo replied, winking at me. He lifted Amal off the ground and carried her to the lounge.

I watched them as they laughed and wrestled playfully before setting up the game.

I could not ask for more, I thought, a warm feeling of bliss taking over my heart.

He was light. A breath of fresh air. The calm after the storm. Your mum tucking in your blankets before sleeping when you were a child. He was the warm embrace of a plush bathrobe after a cold shower. The love that has the power to heal rather than to hurt.

"I love your eyes," Leo told me as we curled up on the sofa after putting Amal to bed. "Even though they run away from me sometimes," he added, looking deep in thought.

---

[26] A quote by German writer Gotthold Ephraim Lessing (1729–1781).

I held his gaze for a few seconds. "If I run away, you *must* get me back," I replied.

"And I *will* get you back. Always," he said without the slightest hint of hesitation, kissing me slowly.

Acknowledgements

This book would have never seen the light of day without the encouragement and support of a bunch of people whom I want to take the time to thank personally.

First, I would like to thank my partner, my daughter, and my sister, who have been both my first and most loyal fans and my harshest critics. There have been times when I felt like giving up, but you spurred me to keep going because, as my little girl would remind me on those occasions: "You should never give up on your dreams."

Thanks to my beloved Mum and Dad, who taught me many things, among which are honesty, intellectual integrity, and the gratification that comes with achieving your goals through determination and hard, honourable work.

I also want to thank the other members of my family who, despite not being directly involved in my creative process, were still with me throughout it. We may live far from each other, but you are always in my thoughts and heart.

A big shout-out to Vicky and Anne-Marie for proofing my first drafts and providing me with precious feedback and guidance.

Special thanks to my publishers Michael Mirolla and Connie McParland, my brilliant editor Françoise Vulpé, and everybody else on the Guernica team for making my biggest dream come true.

I would also like to pay tribute to one of the most inspiring human beings I have met in my life: my mentor Robert Beers, who taught me everything I know about journalism and shared my passion, enthusiasm, and professional values. I hope my words reach you, wherever you are.

Finally, a big thank you to every single person who crossed my path, those who loved me, but also those who didn't. I would not be the person I have become had it not been for each of you. Thank you for providing me with an opportunity to learn about myself, come to terms with my vulnerable side, and appreciate the idiosyncrasies, contradictions, and irony of this amazing, bittersweet journey called life.

About the Author

Valeria Camerino is a UK-based writer, journalist, and globetrotter. She was born in Rome but moved to the North of England when she was nineteen to attend university, and has since settled there. While she has lived and worked in a number of countries, she is particularly fond of Spain and the Arabian Gulf. Valeria is currently working on a collection of short stories that explores gender inequality from a global perspective. In addition to writing, she is passionate about food, flamenco music, foreign cultures, and the human condition. This is her first book.